NOT SO TOP SECRET

The Hart-Ewing Company was a very large installation indeed. It started from scratch with research scientists and experimental labs and grew to the vast structure that created and housed finished pieces of the final products that would eventually take men into space.

Hart-Ewing was an enormous and varied undertaking, and the end results of its functions would have political as well as cultural implications. There were, of course, innumerable avenues for leakage of information—which, in a way, is what made Carson's job as Security Chief so interesting and worthwhile.

So he was understandably put out when he discovered that something was so secure that it was being kept from the Security Chief! Naturally, he had to find out what it was.

TOMORROW IS TOO FAR

James White

A Del Rey Book

BALLANTINE BOOKS • NEW YORK

A Del Rey Book
Published by Ballantine Books

ISBN 0-345-30153-6

Manufactured in the United States of America

First Ballantine Books Edition: February 1971
Second Printing: December 1981

Cover art by Matt Davis

TOMORROW
IS TOO FAR

Chapter 1

The fire had broken out during the early hours of the morning in a supposedly fire-proof storeroom and a small pile of rubbish had been almost completely consumed. Damage to the room was negligible—one of the metal girders supporting the corrugated iron roof was smoke-blackened, as were a few square yards of concrete floor. In itself the incident was unimportant, but it was an important part of Carson's job as Hart-Ewing's chief security officer to discover how and why fires started even when they did no damage.

When he arrived on the scene tense with cold and interrupted sleep, he was assured by everyone concerned it was unimportant and not worth wasting his time over. Carson ignored them politely and firmly. As usual his politeness was misconstrued as weakness and his firmness as a stupid, stubborn streak in an otherwise ineffectual personality so that Carson found himself being called a nosey, petty-minded unprintable, frequently within earshot.

This did not bother him too much because in his opinion a person who was not curious about everything which went on in the world around him might just as well be dead. He had documentation to prove that his birth had been in all respects legitimate, so they were only half right about him.

1

The fire had been discovered by Patrol Officer Sands shortly after one-thirty in the morning. At that time it had almost burnt itself out and Sands had completed the job with his size elevens, so there had been no real reason for the chief security officer to get out of bed. But Carson had wanted to make sure that the incident was as unimportant as it seemed. After taking a quick look around the storeroom he had locked the door, posted Sands outside, and begun to ask questions.

He discovered that the storeroom had been unused for a very long time. The section foreman insisted that someone from another factory—he did not know who—had had it cleared three or four years ago so that they could move material and records into the place, and presumably they still intended doing so because when he asked if he could have it for his own section's use he was always told no, that the space was shortly to be allocated to another section. He added that he did not know who had moved the rubbish into the room and that it must have happened during the early part of the night shift because otherwise some of his operators would have noticed it going in—he promised to ask around, anyway, and let Carson know the result. There was no reason for anyone to go into the place—it was cold, the lights did not work, and if anyone wanted to smoke there was no fire hazard in this area so they were free to do so at the bench.

Carson asked him if he would mind looking at the ashes to see if it was possible to identify, and if possible place the origin of, the rubbish. The foreman did so, shining Carson's flashlight at the acrid-smelling heap for less than a minute, and saying that it could have originated at any one of twenty spots inside this or the other factories, and it was not the sort of rubbish which was burned as a rule—it was simply dumped in the nearest litter bin for collection each morning by the waste disposal people—and that obviously someone was playing some kind of joke because to get to the storeroom the man transporting the stuff would have to pass at least three convenient litter bins. In any case the foreman did not see why Carson was

2

making such a fuss over a pile of burned toffee wrappings, empty cigarette packs, used Kleenex and the like.

It was possible that the man was covering up for someone, but Carson doubted that. His irritation sounded too genuine.

Was there a pyromaniac loose, someone who took great pains to conceal his movements while gathering his tiny hoard of combustibles and even greater care to see that their small conflagration did not spread or do any damage whatever? Could a firebug get his kicks from a small-scale, controlled blaze? The idea *was* ridiculous, so ridiculous that there just had to be a more logical explanation for it.

The rubbish itself was valueless, obviously, because it had been burned. But the burning—now, that was a different matter. A fire could be used for all sorts of things in addition to supplying light and heat . . .

It was at that point that Carson decided to take a really close look at the scene of the crime.

The first thing he noticed was that the upper frames of the storeroom's three small windows had cuphooks screwed into them so that it would need only a few seconds and three pieces of thick sacking for the place to be made light-proof. Two of the pieces of sacking were still in place and if the third had not come adrift from one of its supporting hooks, Sands would not have noticed the fire at all. The blackened area in the center of the floor was larger than he had expected, and closer examination showed that a number of fires had previously occurred on the same area of concrete. The earlier fires had not been reported, of course, because on those occasions the sacking had not slipped and the ashes had probably been moved as covertly as the rubbish had been brought in.

A faint smell of aviation fuel pervaded the place and two small pieces of paper—a lightweight bank normally used for carbon copies—smelled very strongly of it. Both pieces were badly charred, covered by several lines of typing and legible in an area roughly the size and shape of the sole of Sands' boot. The typing contained a great many

3

errors, strike-overs and xxx-ings out, as if the typist was not only unfamiliar with the machine but unused to typing.

Carson's next call was to the area typing pool, where he knew there was a copying machine. He slipped the charred papers between a plastic carrying-sheet and took a photostat copy, left the deserted room as he had found it and returned to the storeroom to replace the two scraps of paper among the ashes. Then he left, dismissing Sands with the remark that he no longer considered the room worth guarding.

Sands was a trifle vehement in his agreement.

Irritated, Carson said, "You are on duty until mid-day, I understand. When the day shift comes on I want you to do a little detective work. This area is badly lit and practically deserted late at night, but earlier there are a lot of people not specifically engaged on night work but tacking a few hours' overtime on to the end of their day shift, and these people may have noticed something. You are to ask them if they saw an electric truck carrying two or three full litter bins moving around this section last night and if they know the driver's name. Got that?"

"Yes, sir," said Sands patiently.

"I'm going back to the office now—it's too late to go back to bed. Ring me there as soon as you have anything to report . . ."

A few minutes later Carson let himself into his office, locked the door carefully and quietly behind him, and went to his desk. The bottom left-hand drawer was slightly warped and difficult to open but it was not locked—a fact which should, he hoped, indicate that it contained nothing of value. There was a drawer very like it in most desks, regardless of the neatness and efficiency of the occupant. It was the drawer reserved for junk.

In Carson's case it contained a couple of old girlie magazines belonging to his six-years-gone predecessor, a quantity of picture postcards with the stamps cut off—his secretary had a philatelist nephew—a pair of old shoes, and a fossilized sandwich. At the bottom there was a large

4

padded envelope of the kind used to send books through the post. It was torn and scribbled on and bore a large number of brown circles made by overfull coffee cups.

Without removing it from the drawer, Carson opened the envelope and withdrew a slim, clean, foolscap file to which he added the photostats he had just taken. There were only a few pages in the file, most of them containing lists of requisition numbers and drawing reference numbers which did not quite fit any of the company's current projects. Another page was covered with neat calculations concerning the time taken by a body accelerating at ninety-six feet per second to travel a distance of 2,376,000 miles, thrust being applied only during the first and final fifteen minutes of the journey.

But the two new items were the first to actually *say* anything. One of the charred scraps had said

> *Available measuring instruments incapable of differentiating between instantaneous and the velocity of light over this distance. Five weeks real time required to reach ... of plus trip home. Theoretically it is possible to reach the systems of Tau Ceti and ... ately the return journey is impossible with existing power sources and until we understand the ... try jumps of a few hours in the minus direction only. The philosophical implications need careful investigation before the two-way sequence is attempted. Biological effects and structural damage to the brain is negligible with lab ... a human subject able to report on the psychological side-effects on his return so that ... MMIT TO MEMORY AND DESTROY AT ONCE.*

Whoever they were and whatever it was, they were extremely Security-conscious.

The second scrap was covered by handwritten calculations where someone had multiplied two hundred and fifteen by three hundred and sixty and then by twenty-four and used the rest of the sheet to doodle.

5

Carson replaced the file in its padded envelope, rearranged the junk over it, closed the drawer and unlocked his office door. The paperwork was piled high on his IN tray and he really should take this opportunity of clearing some of it. But he could not concentrate. His stomach was bothering him.

He did not feel sick exactly—it felt a little like indigestion, or hunger, or that unpleasantly gone sensation so inadequately described as butterflies in the stomach. He realized suddenly that he was feeling excitement so intense that it was actually painful.

What was going on .. ?

As a rule Carson was kept too busy to be bored, but at the same time his work could never by any stretch of the imagination be called exciting. That was why he took such a keen interest in everything that went on—even though a great many people detested him for it—and it was the reason why he had become even more curious when he discovered something going on which was, if not actually wrong, at least highly unusual.

It had begun when he chanced to hear a couple of operators belly-aching happily at their benches. The men had been discussing the components they were making, suggesting that somebody up top had boobed because the part they were producing did not quite fit the sub-assembly they were making it for, and complaining about the moral cowardice of the section chief because he would not listen to them because apparently *his* chief did not want to know.

Even if what the men said had been true, it represented a very small wastage of the operator's time in relation to the enormous output of the company as a whole, and in any case it was a job for the efficiency experts. But then Carson had discovered similar wastage and inefficiency occurring in a number of sharply defined areas in several factories. Mistakes, the same mistakes down to the last millimeter, were being made over and over again and being either ignored or covered up.

The mistakes it became clear to Carson, were being very carefully planned.

He had taken to working late two or three times a week, choosing the nights at random and tramping through the various buildings which had lights burning, ostensibly to check on the efficiency of his own men. Without, of course, being able to join them, he had discovered liaison meetings in progress between engineers and design staff, some of whom had nothing in common to liaise about, and an occasional production meeting which went on for hours without using or producing minutes or paperwork of any kind. Even the wastepaper baskets contained only a few empty cigarette cartons.

Paperwork, the proof that something was in fact going on, was virtually non-existent except for his pitifully small list of drawing issue notes, materials requisition forms and the like bearing the identifying numbers of the suspect components. Carson knew that *something* was going on but he did not know what it was or whether it was small, medium or large as projects went. He still did not know exactly, but today's discovery had rendered his ignorance less abysmal.

It had to do with space travel, perhaps a new method of propulsion effective over interstellar distances. And it was important—there could be no doubt about that—and secret. So secret that even the Ewing-Hart security section had been kept in the dark about it.

But even as a child Carson had never been comfortable in the dark.

Chapter 2

"This is ridiculous!" said Carson irritably to Chief Patrol Officer Donovan, who was standing at attention on the other side of the desk. "What made you think it important enough to warrant an S-Eight form and what the blazes did the man do—what *could* he do in that place!—to make his department head want us to run a second security check on him? And sit down, George. Relax. Is the new job he applied for in an unusually sensitive area?"

"Airframe fatigue testing on the stretched HE93, sir," said Donovan quickly, using Carson's pause for breath to dispose of one of the questions. He sat, arms and legs arranged neatly, erect, comfortable and somehow still at attention. The late morning sunlight struck down at him like a golden spotlight, its light and heat almost completely absorbed by the thick, dark serge of his uniform.

"There is nothing secret about the HE93," said Carson drily. "Their paperwork isn't even Restricted. Why the S-Eight?"

Donovan blinked steadily for a few seconds, a sure sign that he was marshaling facts, then said, "Three days ago I was stopped by Mr. Silverman. Among other things he mentioned that one of his men, Mr. Pebbles, had applied for a job in another department. He seemed to treat this as a great joke, but suggested that a man like Pebbles should not be allowed to move freely within the company because he was God's gift to a Russian agent. Mr. Silverman laughed a lot at his own suggestion. As you know, sir, he laughs practically all the time.

"Yesterday he stopped me again and talked for about twenty minutes," Donovan went on. "During this period he mentioned Pebbles on five separate occasions, repeating what he had said earlier and adding that while Pebbles was one of the nicest people you could meet he was incapable of keeping his mouth shut. Mr. Silverman made it plain that he did not think the man Pebbles was a security risk, but the man was little more than an organic tape-recorder who played back to anyone on request, and the security department should be officially notified of the situation.

"That is why I made out the S-Eight, sir," Donovan concluded. "I think it's ridiculous, too."

Carson was silent for a moment while he stared at Donovan and thought. The office window had jammed again and the place was like an oven, but the other man sat there in his impossibly neat uniform with its quietly impressive rows of service ribbons, steady-eyed, firm-jawed and without a visible drop of perspiration on him. Probably he had a grown family, a fondness for gardening and a pair of comfortable old slacks at home, but Carson could not imagine him in anything else but a uniform or doing anything which was not strictly according to regulations.

"You did the right thing, George," he said finally. "Since the matter has been brought officially to my attention I must do, or at least appear to do, something about it. Was there anything else . . . ?"

When the senior patrol officer had gone the thought occurred to him that all this might simply be a buildup to one of Silverman's jokes—an unusually elaborate one designed, perhaps, to make Carson look ridiculous. But initiating proceedings to carry out a security re-check on any employee was not something to be done as a joke. The proce-

9

dure was much more thorough and wide-ranging than that carried out for a simple pre-employment check. As well as the long and costly investigation with its intensive surveillance and invasion of privacy, the implications for the man concerned were, to say the very least, serious . . .

The telephone derailed his train of thought, but only temporarily because it was Silverman.

"Think of the Devil," said Carson drily, then went on, "Ted, I want to talk to you about the masterspy you're harboring in your department . . . "

Silverman laughed uproariously for several seconds before gaining control of the paroxysm with evident difficulty. He said, "Joe, you'll be the death of me! Masterspy, haha. Obviously Donovan has been talking to you. Donovan is a good man, Joe, seriously. Conscientious, keen— maybe too keen, but that really isn't a fault now, is it? I barely mentioned Pebbles to him, you know, but he jumped at it—practically bayed like a bloodhound—and insisted on making out an official report. Wish I had a few keen people like that in my department . . . "

Carson tried to imagine Donovan baying like a bloodhound or telling a lie and could do neither. Somebody was bending the truth.

" . . . But I didn't mean him to take it *that* seriously," Silverman was saying. "Pebbles is a good man, Joe. Hardworking. If he gets this new job I'll be sorry to lose him, but I like to see people of his kind bettering themselves. Within limits, of course . . . "

"Is he colored?"

Silverman laughed again. "Are you suggesting I'm a racist, Joe? No, he's white, and the matter isn't all that important. But I don't think we should discuss it over the phone. Security, you know." He had another paroxysm of mirth which he switched off suddenly to add, "I'll see you at lunch. And Joe, don't forget to bring your cigarette lighter-shaped tape-recorder . . . "

"Lunch it is," said Carson, hanging up on the inevitable laughter.

Before returning to his paperwork Carson paused for a few minutes to wonder what it was about Pebbles that was so unimportant yet urgent. Was it possible that Silverman was on to something—something so tenuous or circumstantial that he risked making a fool of himself by reporting it directly? Carson doubted it. At the same time he could not help thinking that it would be nice if, just once, he could catch himself a spy.

Carson stared at his heaped IN tray without seeing it, sighed and slipped into his favorite daydream.

It need not be a Fuchs or a Pontecorvo or even one of the professionals for whom the other side would be willing to swap a couple of imprisoned amateurs. He would settle for a simple case of passing on classified information for sale to the newspapers or another company. If he could even interrupt a minor act of sabotage and apprehend the culprit, that would satisfy him and serve to make people take his department and himself just a little more seriously.

Carson knew that he was not taken seriously and neither was his department. He was treated by the majority of the company's twelve thousand-odd personnel with a mixture of amusement, irritation and dislike—the ingredients varying in strength and quantity in direct relation to his activities at the time—while his men were looked on as something between members of the company Gestapo and characters out of Gilbert and Sullivan.

They were the stupid, petty-minded officials who refused to allow a boy who had scarcely begun to shave to visit his girl during lunch-break in another part of the factory, just because his identity tag did not have the proper endorsements. When the level of pilfering rose above acceptable limits, they subjected the workers to the monstrous indignity of opening the trunks of their cars, causing a traffic pile-up at the gates and making everyone late for tea. And if a couple of windows were left open or a door left unlocked or, best of all, a cigarette left smoldering, the members of Carson's Gestapo would become quite shrewish and a memo dripping with verbal acid would arrive on the department head's desk first thing next morning . . .

As usual, Carson thought angrily, his daydream was turning into a nightmare. The real source of his trouble lay in the fact that, despite the aura of authority, danger and intrigue which was supposed to surround a chief security officer, he had one of the most boring jobs imaginable. He knew this and accepted it most of the time.

But sometimes he seemed to find it necessary to manufacture and chase wills-of-the-wisp like the ultra-secret space drive project he had uncovered. Probably there was a simple explanation for the evidence he had found—provided it was considered separately, item by item, and not twisted into fantastic shapes to make it all fit together.

Angrily he reached for the first item in his tray, determined to tranquilize himself with an overdose of routine. It was an application for permission to visit the guided weapons production line, the rocket engine test area and the module assembly building by a reporter and photographer from one of the dailies. The purpose of the visit was stated as gathering material for an illustrated feature on the Hart-Ewing contribution to the nation's aerospace industry. Simpson of the publicity department would escort the two newsmen during the visit.

The missile which they wanted to see being produced had sold to so many different countries that the only thing secret about it was the name of the next customer, and the country concerned had already leaked that for political reasons. The rocket engine test area did not worry him either—there was nothing to see but a lot of unclassified smoke and flames. In the module assembly area there were a few places which would have to be avoided for reasons of commercial rather than military security, certain processes which should not be photographed.

Simpson was aware of these places and would co-operate by avoiding them. Unlike Simpson, the majority of people at Hart-Ewing's did not co-operate or volunteer information or offer helpful advice to the security department. That was why Carson was becoming so curious about the Pebbles business.

Curious but not suspicious.

Chapter 3

When he arrived for lunch Silverman was nowhere in sight, but Bill Savage was sitting at an otherwise empty table for four so he joined him. A few minutes later Savage said, "Please do."

Carson grinned and said, "Thank you. I'm expecting company but before he comes I wonder if you could give me some information about an employee. I should ask one of your clerks instead of bothering you with it, but this isn't official—I'm simply curious. The man's name is Pebbles."

Savage had been watching his face while he spoke, but suddenly he looked down at his plate. From experience Carson knew that the Personnel officer was not avoiding his eyes through embarrassment or guilt or because he was about to tell a lie—Savage was not that kind of man. It was just that when a person or thing offended him he tried not to look at it. Carson, apparently, had become offensive.

"This seems to be my week," he said finally, "for being asked unofficial questions about Mr. Pebbles. What do you want to know, and whose side are you on?"

"I don't know, to both questions," Carson replied. "I'd just like to know what all the fuss is about."

Savage nodded and looked up. He said, "His name is

John Pebbles. Unmarried. Age about thirty. Medically fit but mentally somewhat retarded. We accepted him because it is company policy to employ a proportion of disabled persons on our work force. For the past three years he has been doing odd jobs, mostly fetching and carrying and sweeping floors in various factories. Now he has applied for a clerical position in another department and unless something happens to mess things up for him the grapevine says he'll get it."

"I see," said Carson. "Is his present job difficult or unpleasant .. ?"

"Let's say it lacks status," said Silverman, laughing as he joined them. Savage stared silently at the remains of his steak.

"Seriously, Bill," Silverman went on, "you really should go a bit easier on your 'Opportunities for Advancement' speech when you're processing new employees—especially an obvious half-wit like Pebbles. Probably you feel sorry for him and would like to see him get on. The feeling does you credit, but let's face it, Bill, Pebbles is not quite right in the head. You are in danger of making a simple-minded, basically happy man thoroughly discontented and unhappy . . . "

Silverman was fairly radiating sincerity, but he rather spoiled the effect by addressing Carson as if he was a member of a jury rather than Savage.

" . . . With me he is doing a job well within his capabilities. Now, that is. In the early days he pulled some really stupid stunts, like trying to ride an electric truck down two flights of stairs just because some other nitwit dared him to do it. Only I was sorry for him, and he had managed to make friends in high places who asked me to let him stay so—"

"Who," said Carson suddenly, "asked you to let him stay?"

Silverman became less genial at being put off his stride. "Oh, Tillotson, Reece, a couple of people from the design office—until then I didn't know they knew he existed. Maybe they were sorry for him, too, or maybe he isn't as

15

half-witted as he pretends. He certainly isn't grateful—I gave him the job in the first place, kept him when he didn't know left from right, trained him until he has become completely dependable, and now I'm going to lose one of my best men because you, Bill, are too soft-hearted to treat men the way they should be treated in a big organization like this one, as productive units to be deployed with the greatest possible efficiency.

"You know, Bill," Silverman ended with a great, bellowing laugh, "I sometimes think you should get a job in the MacNaughton Clinic where you can help handicapped people all the time . . . What's wrong, Bill?"

"I think I'll skip dessert," said Savage, throwing his paper napkin at his half-finished lunch.

When he had gone Silverman laughed and said, "I think Bill takes things too seriously. Pebbles isn't so important that people in our position should quarrel about him. At the same time I don't think he should move to another department—"

"My interest," said Carson stiffly, "is purely in the security aspect . . . "

Silverman wagged his head in amusement. "Joe, now *you're* taking things too seriously. You can handle this quietly and unofficially. Pebbles isn't a Commie or anything—he hasn't enough brains to think political thoughts! —and Donovan dramatizes things. It is just that he is so gullible and childish that if he were to find out anything of a confidential nature he would tell it to the first person he met. His foot is permanently in his mouth . . . "

"Sounds like an interesting character," said Carson. "I'm looking forward to seeing him."

Silverman shook his head. "No need for that now, you understand the position. We are more realistic about these things, than is Bill. This really is the best thing for Pebbles, you'll see.

"By the way," he added. "I didn't see your car outside. Can I give you a lift back?"

Carson did not reply at once. He was thinking that this was not a security matter and that it was an indication of

16

how Silverman regarded Carson and his department that he would use it simply to keep a good if not particularly bright worker from moving out of his section. Carson had yet to meet Pebbles but he already knew where his sympathies lay.

"I'm putting on weight," he said suddenly. "I'll walk..."

On the way back to the office he stopped for a moment to watch a production EH93, its violent yellow paint job indicating that it had just come off the line and had still to be given its customer livery, warming up its engines. He noted with approval that two of his crash tenders were already in position on the edge of the runway, their rotating beacons winking dully in the bright sunshine. But he did not stay to watch the take-off. Despite the sun there was a cold wind blowing across the airfield and he had been stupid to refuse that lift.

On his return to the Admin building his first call was at Personnel to ask Bill Savage for Pebbles' location and a copy of his dossier. "I want to see him as soon as possible," he went on. "And look at me, dammit! I'm on your side, but I still have to go through the motions."

Savage looked up and nodded. "I'm glad. But treat him gently, Joe. He isn't exactly as Laughing Boy described him."

Pebbles worked in the large, bright room which was the nerve center—if such a hypothetical plant could be said to possess one—of the company grapevine. The gory details of an accident to one of the operators in Factory Three, the latest news of a Government missile contract, the *real* reason behind an impending strike of riveters and a truly shocking—in both senses of the word—quantity of scandal was the type of up-to-date and surprisingly accurate information constantly available in this room. Because of the overwhelming urge in most people to gossip and to impress each other with the quality of confidential information to which they were privy, the room was, from the Security standpoint, about as porous as a rabbit hutch. At times it was Carson's biggest single headache and some of

17

the names he called it were neither polite nor printable, although the sign on the door read simply MALE STAFF TOILET.

Carson did not look at Pebbles until he was washing his hands. He had chosen a washbasin near enough for easy conversation but not so close that it would hamper the other's work.

Pebbles was dressed in neat blue overalls. Two highly polished but badly tied shoes projected from the lower ends and a clean collar and tie showed at the top. The tie had a quiet but distinctive pattern on it and the limp, slightly frayed appearance of a status symbol worn with pride but perhaps a little too often. Carson had a tie just like it at home. Pebbles was mopping the tiled floor and whistling part of the third movement from Rimsky-Korsakov's *Scheherazade* and doing both with enthusiasm.

Taking a deep breath, Carson said pleasantly, "I prefer the last movement myself. Especially the ending—you know, where the solo violin holds that very high note. It's so high I sometimes think my neighbor's dog is the only one able to appreciate it."

He stopped, waiting for the other's reaction.

Pebbles looked up quickly but did not speak. His expression reflected an odd mixture of pleasure, confusion and wariness—the expression, perhaps, of one who is uncertain whether he is being praised or having his leg pulled. His features did not seem to be those of an idiot—the face had an innocent rather than a vacant look. It was the look of a child—a child with problems, perhaps, but not necessarily a stupid child. Carson tried again.

"I hear that you may be going to a new job soon. You're looking forward to that, I expect . . . "

Pebbles began to stammer and for several interminable seconds nothing came out. Carson had spent some time thinking about his approach and subsequent treatment of Pebbles. He had not wanted to unsettle or frighten the man nor did he want their meeting to appear contrived. He knew that children were sensitive to any trace of condescension or insincerity on the part of adults trying to communicate with them, and presumably people with childish or retarded minds would have a similar sensitivity. Rather than being guilty of condescension Carson felt that he had gone too far in the opposite direction by projecting the conversation several yards above the poor slob's head.

In any case he had come simply to satisfy his curiosity enough about the man to be able to move Donovan's report from the IN to the OUT tray marked "No Action Required." The whole business was becoming downright embarassing for both Pebbles and himself. Obviously he was wasting his time trying to start a conversation with the man and he had, after all, more important things to do.

Carson turned to go. He said, "I . . . ah . . . hope you do well in the job . . . "

Pebbles was staring at him, still trying to speak, his expression apologetic and determined. He seemed to be apologizing for the barrier that would not let his words come through and determined that they were going to get through anyway—he reminded Carson of a child given a difficult word to spell. Finally he succeeded.

"I . . . I can do multiplication and division," he said, very proudly, "and I've been able to do joined-up writing, not block capitals, for over two years. I can work out a triangle of velocities and calculate . . . "

"That's good," said Carson, patting him on the shoulder as he headed for the door. He was wondering what a triangle of velocities was and how Pebbles had come by that tie.

Chapter 4

The telephone was ringing when he returned to the office. It was Sands reporting that just before he was due to go off duty he had spoken to the man responsible for moving the waste to the storeroom.

" . . . Before talking to him," Sands went on briskly, "I checked his clock card for last night. He clocked out nearly three hours before the fire was reported and so could not have been directly responsible for it. However, he admitted to working late and to moving a load of waste to the storeroom in response to a telephone call from Production Control. He also said that he had heard about the fire but had not realized that it had been in that particular storeroom. He did not appear to be worried about the incident and he certainly did not look guilty. His name is Pebbles and if you were to speak to him, sir, you would understand why I don't suspect him of—"

"I already have, and do," said Carson, unable to resist the temptation of stealing the other's thunder. "But you've done very well. Go on, please."

"Yes, sir. When I questioned him further about the telephone call . . . "

Sands went on to say that the voice had sounded pleasant but authoritative, it had identified its department of origin but not itself, and it had asked Pebbles if he would not mind emptying the litter bins in Production Control and transferring their contents to a certain storeroom in Factory Three. Apparently one of the PC girls had lost the stone of her engagement ring and wanted a chance to search the litter thoroughly before the waste disposal people took it away. Pebbles had been asked to avoid factory personnel as much as possible and speak to no one on the way because the girl concerned did not want to have her leg pulled about it.

Pebbles added that he had been asked to do the same exercise for different departments on a great many occasions for very similar reasons, and suggested that the girl looking for her property might have been smoking at the time and the stub or ash could have smoldered for hours before setting fire to the waste.

Nobody in Production Control admitted either to losing valuables or asking to have their litter moved, Sands said, but in the circumstances that was to be expected. Sands thought the whole affair was stupid and childish—the company did not know how lucky it was that the waste had not been moved to an empty refueling bay!—but it explained everything and it was so ridiculous that it was almost certainly the true explanation.

Carson agreed that it was very neat, thanked him for staying late to report and rang off. He got up from his desk, walked to the window and stared out across the busy airfield without seeing a thing.

The man who had phoned Pebbles had not, of course, belonged to Production Control. He had *said* so, but the call could have originated at any one of the eight hundred-odd internal telephone extensions within the Hart-Ewing complex. That same man, or one of his colleagues, would know by now that the fire had been put out rather than being allowed to burn itself out. He would also know that a member of Carson's comic Gestapo had been asking questions and that Security now knew that the waste had been moved to the storeroom. But he did *not* know whether the material he had wanted destroyed by the burning waste had been burned or not.

The question now was whether he or his friends would risk going back to the storeroom to make sure. If there really was a Most Secret project being worked on at Hart-Ewing—if Carson had not been working himself into a lather of excitement over a list of mis-copied figures and some author/engineer's plot notes for a science-fiction story—the answer was that they most certainly would.

Assuming the existence of such a project, there could be no doubt at all that the people concerned were very security-conscious regarding their activities and paperwork. They could not risk sending Pebbles to check on the situation—apparently the man was incapable either of telling a lie or concealing a fact—so the chances were that one of the project personnel would be sent to check for himself. If they were really worried it would be as soon as possible —tonight, in fact.

Carson went to the wide, flat drawer built into the top of his triple filing cabinet and withdrew a large-scale drawing of Factory Three. As well as giving the positions of walls, partitions and storerooms it showed the power and lighting cable runs, high pressure air supplies, fire pumps and emergency exits. He studied it carefully for several minutes, looking for a good hiding place. His problem was complicated by the fact that he did not want to trap a man, just have a good look at him without the other realizing it. He replaced the drawing, looked at his watch, and began to compose a memo to the chief maintenance engineer.

In it he drew attention to the recent fire and suggested that the power, lighting and internal telephone lines in the section should be checked immediately for possible damage. He knew that if he waited until late afternoon before sending it the internal postal system would not deliver it until early next morning, so that the maintenance people could not send an electrician to check the area tonight. But the memo would have today's date on it and, if someone later became worried about lights flashing on and off all around them, it should stand up to a perfunctory investigation well enough to reassure the culprit.

The disquieting thought occurred to him that the man

was not a culprit, a saboteur, or a wrong-doer of any kind. Instead he was on Carson's side, helping guard a secret so important that the chief security officer had not been made aware of it. With that thought came another which suggested that Carson had no business poking his nose into the affair and would be serving the best interests of his country and his company by letting it drop.

He did want to serve the best interests of his country, and of the company which entrusted him with its internal and external security. He knew that he was good at the job —conscientious, meticulous, exacting where even the relatively unimportant details were concerned, so much so that in certain quarters he was described as a fussy old woman. But *was* he considered good at his job by the people who really mattered, Carson asked himself suddenly, or merely as a nosey old woman whose curiosity about everyone and everything rendered his ability to keep his own mouth shut suspect? Was that the real reason he was being kept in the dark?

That was the most disquieting thought of all. Carson tried to force it out of his mind by concentrating on his paperwork. He was so successful in this that he could not afterwards remember the composition of the sandwiches he had had sent in at quitting time. But much later that evening, when he was sitting on a hard and very cold toolbox in Factory Three with only the top of his head showing above a nearby bench, the thought recurred. This time there was no way of avoiding it.

Either he was good at this job or he was not. If he was not then the company would have eased him out before now—they would not wait six years before deciding whether or not he was efficient. And if he was fulfilling his function as a security officer, then it could be argued that his duties included the protection of any and all secret work in which Hart-Ewing was engaged, that it was his duty to protect it even when he had no real idea what "it" was all about.

Carson sighed. Around him the metal benches and structural supports creaked and tinkled faintly as they gave up the heat of the working day. The night shift at the other end of the section contributed its quiet clangor and the kittens, who were the furry debris of the continuing population explosion among the factory cats, romped among the now safe and silent machinery.

Security and counter-espionage, so far as Carson was concerned, was far from being an exciting and glamorous job. Security meant checking fire extinguishers and hoses, checking lights and doors left on or open, checking safety precautions during aircraft refueling, checking pilfering when it began to assume the proportions of grand larceny, checking trespassers on other people's parking spaces, checking everything everywhere several times a day or week.

Counter-espionage did not, on the other hand, mean a constant war against industrial or foreign spies who were bending every effort to penetrate the company's security defenses with cuff-link cameras and sub-miniaturized electronic devices. Instead, it involved a constant round of checking doors, drawers and lock-up filing cabinets to make sure that classified material was returned to its proper place and not left lying around where any one of the cleaning or night maintenance staffs, decorators or telephone repairmen could see it. In short, Carson's job lay not so much in defending his company's secrets as to try to prevent their being given away.

He even had his own *Index Expurgatoria* of forbidden photographs and subjects which operated in reverse to keep over-enthusiastic Sales and Publicity people from rushing into print with classified material in the technical journals.

But security on this special project was tight and professional—the men concerned made none of the usual mistakes and Carson had had to go to a lot of trouble even to satisfy himself that a project actually existed. He was still not completely sure that it did exist. Their planning was superb and when they had to act openly they did so tracelessly by making use of someone like Pebbles, a nice,

24

simple-minded obliging man who believed everything he was told.

Quite a lot of people seemed to have a use for Pebbles, Carson thought angrily. He was remembering how proud the man had looked when he said that he could do joined-up writing. Pebbles would have been fired on at least two occasions if someone with influence had not spoken for him. The thought that Pebbles had been kept in the company and used by these people as a sort of organic, un-thinking tool did not make Carson feel as the same thought would have made Bill Savage, but it made him feel a mo-ment of shame because he was considering making use of him as well, to help him find out something about the pur-poses of the people who were already using him . . .

Carson's mind froze suddenly in mid-thought. Someone was coming, a dim figure approaching his hiding place along the aisle between the storeroom outer wall and the ranks of silent machines. In the light which filtered across from the active side of the factory floor he could see that the man wore a cap and overalls. They were not white overalls nor were they the dark blue, green or brown shades worn by inspectors, laborers, apprentices or elec-tricians, but some medium color which he could not iden-tify in the darkness. He kept his eyes on the man while his hand went to the panel of light switches beside him.

One hundred yards away a group of roof lights blinked on and off several times and a few seconds later a section even farther away was erratically illuminated in similar fashion. The man had stopped dead when the first lights went on, but they were too far away to show Carson his face and in any case he was merely getting the man used to the idea that lights were being tested in the area. He watched the man hurry silently to the storeroom door and close it behind him.

An intermittent glow showed in the uncovered window as he used a flashlight, then disappeared as the sacking which had dropped from the window was replaced. Per-haps ten minutes later the man came out again.

This time Carson made sure that the lights which flicked

on and off again were close enough to make identification positive.

The face revealed was that of Wayne Tillotson! He was wearing, not overalls, but a flying suit of pale grey which was almost the same shade as his face at that moment. Carson switched off the overhead lights and played with the other switches at random until Tillotson had gone.

In the storeroom a few minutes later he used his own flashlight to study the pile of ashes. The two scraps of oil-soaked paper which he had copied and replaced earlier had gone and a few of the ashes were again warm.

Tillotson had been one of the people who had used his influence to keep Pebbles from being fired, although why the company's chief test pilot should have concerned himself with the fate of a lavatory attendant was something which still required a full explanation. At that moment Carson decided quite definitely that he would get to know, cultivate, and as soon as possible use Pebbles. Everyone else seemed to be doing it.

He was still thinking about the best way of doing so as he went to the area telephone and began ringing around the gatehouses and patrol offices.

Chapter 5

The questions were too many and too general to arouse suspicion among his own patrolmen—he had used his fussy, chronic worrier's voice. But from them he discovered that some kind of meeting was going on in the office of the Chief of Design on the third floor of the Admin building and that the chief test pilot's unmistakable bone-shaker was parked outside.

Carson was there ten minutes later asking more fussy, seemingly unconnected questions.

"I don't know who is in there or how many, sir," the patrolman in charge told him. "When Briggs looked in during his early rounds he said the ashtrays were full and the wastebaskets empty. Maybe they are playing cards . . ."

"Are you being sarcastic?" began Carson, but he was interrupted by Patrolman Briggs from the other side of the office.

"One of the men was Mr. Daniels, sir," he said quickly, while his eyes shouted, *Shut up, you fool—can't you see he's in one of his moods tonight?* He went on, "Mr. Daniels was writing on the blackboard. The others had their backs turned to me so I couldn't see who they were—except for Mr. Tillotson, of course, who left the meeting about half an hour ago and came back shortly before you arrived."

"Any idea of what they were doing?"

"No, sir. Mr. Daniels was talking while he wrote on the board but stopped when he saw me. He had been saying something about the major problems on a minus trip home being largely psychological. Yes, that was exactly what he said. The diagrams and math on the blackboard I couldn't understand at all."

Carson nodded approval. "At least you keep your eyes and ears open, even when there is nothing to see or hear."

"It's breaking up now, sir," Briggs said, jerking his thumb at the office window and the corridor beyond. "They're coming out of the elevator."

There were only six of them. Somehow Carson had been expecting more than that. But they were all top people: Tillotson, capless now and wearing a topcoat over his flying suit so that the blue-grey gabardine visible below it might easily have been ordinary sports slacks; Dreamy Daniels, the Design chief; the Head of Electronics George Reece; Brady and Soames from module production side and Reg Saunderson, the company chief accountant. It was Daniels who tossed the bunch of keys to Briggs and wished him good night. They did not appear to notice Carson, whose face was above the cone of light thrown out by the desk lamp.

As Briggs was returning the keys to their numbered peg Carson forestalled him. "I'll take them. It's time for rounds and I need some exercise."

Briggs nodded and moved to accompany him. He said, "That bunch are usually very good at switching off lights and locking doors and windows—we haven't caught them out in nearly three years."

"That's what I like to hear," said Carson. "But I can do without your company. You two make some coffee and talk about me behind my back until I get back. In case you've forgotten, I like it black with three lumps and . . . "

" . . . Two plain biscuits," said Briggs, grinning.

Carson had chosen to walk up to the design office, not because he needed the exercise but because at this time of night the elevator could be heard all over the building and, if it was not heard while he was supposedly moving from floor to floor, the two patrol officers might wonder if something was wrong. As things were, they would be expecting him to check all the floors on foot and would not expect to hear the elevator until just before his return to the office. And if they needed him for something they, being somewhat elderly and beefy individuals, would come looking for him in the elevator, which would give plenty of warning of their approach.

He was intending to spend all of the available time in the design office.

All the windows, filing cabinets and wastebaskets in Daniels' office were secured, locked and empty, respectively. No documents had chanced to fall behind or between the office furniture, no used sheets of carbon paper were lying balled-up and unnoticed in a corner, and there were no scratch pads lying around which showed indentations from the writing on preceeding pages. But on the long, baize-topped conference table near the freshly-cleaned blackboard there was a crisp, neatly folded drawing whose reference number and title were partially obscured by the overflow from an ashtray.

Three cigarette butts and a small quantity of ash had spilled on to the drawing and the baize. There seemed to be a strange hint of order to this untidiness, in the positioning of the butts, the ash and the angle made by the drawing against the edge of the table.

The cleaning staff for this particular building had long since gone home, so there would be nobody here to tidy up until tomorrow when Daniels unlocked his office.

Carson examined the drawing as closely as possible without touching it or allowing his breath to disturb the spilled ash, then he sat down carefully in one of the chairs to think.

He could not be absolutely sure that the drawing and ashtray setup was a trap, but his certainty was as close to one hundred percent as made no difference. That being the case, he had to decide whether the trap had been set merely as a precaution or because they thought someone—perhaps Carson himself—was on to them. Again he could not be sure, but he seriously doubted the latter possibility.

Having Sands question Pebbles about the transfer of the waste to the storeroom was the sort of thing expected of Carson, just as he was expected to fuss and ask questions about the fire for weeks afterwards. The unexpected things he had done—the long-term and heavily disguised inquiries, the business with the lights tonight when he had identified Tillotson, and his presence here in Daniels' office —were not yet known to them. The reason for the trap might simply be Tillotson's recent fright.

It would be interesting to see if they continued to set traps after they had an opportunity of seeing his memo to the electricians . . .

All at once Carson felt an overwhelming, angry impatience with the whole stupid project. He *knew* there was something important going on and that it was his duty to know about it. He dearly wanted to question Daniels, Tillotson and the others directly—he was sure that he knew enough to stampede them into telling him the whole story. After all, a project of this importance needed a security officer.

Or did it . . . ?

The thought that somewhere in the company there was a shadow security officer, someone charged with the protection of the really valuable and important work, someone whose organization might take a very poor view of Carson prying into something which was not his concern made him feel frightened as well as angry and inadequate.

Who was the other security man and which organization did he represent? Certainly he was, if he existed at all, operating outside the security department Carson headed.

This *was* his business and whether they wanted it or not they would have his protection. Carson wriggled uncomfortably in the chair and began to consider the anatomy of a project, any project.

At the top were the men responsible for the original idea or for developing someone else's original idea. In the middle were the people who helped break down the idea into large numbers of detail drawings and the engineers who decided how best to convert these drawings into three dimensional metal on someone's bench. In this age of over-specialization it was not expected that the man who produced the detail hardware should understand, or even care about, the part his particular chunk of hardware played in the project as a whole.

But somewhere within the vast Hart-Ewing complex hardware for this ultra-secret project was being made, modified, re-made and sometimes scrapped—there were always teething troubles with a new project, even the relatively simple and non-secret ones. Carson did not think he would get very far questioning the men at the bottom— there were too many thousands of them. A better bet would be the middle men, the engineers and draftsmen who had to iron out the bugs and generally see that all the pieces fitted together. They should be able to help him, except that all the indications were that they also were unaware of what was really going on. There were too many middle men to keep a secret of this magnitude, so they were being used and subtly misdirected by the people at the top, just as Pebbles had been used, but on a more impersonal level.

The idea, he had already decided, was to use the people they were using to find out what they were using them for . . .

As he was switching off the lights and relocking the doors, he had to remind himself again that Daniels and the others were not the Other Side. Neither were they careless. They did their own typing, they did not leave project paperwork lying around, and they went to a great deal of trouble to destroy that which they did not, for some reason, burn in the privacy of their homes. He wondered suddenly if the material was so sensitive that they dared not risk taking it off company limits because of the very slight possibility that one of them might have a car accident while carrying it.

Could it be as secret as *that*?

By the time he returned to the patrol office he felt so

31

impatient that it was an effort to chat with his men while he drank their coffee. Outside the night was clear and cold and full of stars.

He wondered which one of them was Tau Ceti.

Chapter 6

"Waste," said Herbie Patterson, "sheer waste. Somebody gives somebody a bum figure and hundreds of the things are made before somebody else catches on. If I had a tenth of the money wasted in this place in a year I could live in luxury for the next fifty ..."

Carson doubted that but he nodded agreement anyway. Herbie Patterson was a very conscientious and able clerical supervisor who expected everyone else to be the same. The fact that they weren't had soured his disposition over the years until now he was the biggest sorehead in the company. But only his wife and a few people at Hart-Ewing knew about his heart condition and that he had more to gripe about than even he realized.

Herbie never really understood why he had been allocated a parking space only twenty-five yards from his office when the usual distance between parking slot and place of employment was nearer half a mile, but it had made him Carson's friend for life.

Taking advantage of that friendship made Carson feel like a particularly obnoxious form of ghoul.

"... The material wasted, made up to wrong specs and scrapped during the past few years ... You just wouldn't believe it, Joe."

"Try me," said Carson.

"It's a complicated business. To understand what has been going on you would really have had to observe the temporary bouts of insanity which periodically overtake our masters—some of our masters, that is. The ones who spend fifty-one weeks in the year counting pennies and one week chucking thousands down the drain!"

"Are you bitching about your immediate lord and master, or lords and masters generally?" said Carson, forcing a tone of indifference into his voice. Herbie's immediate superior was Reg Saunderson, the company's chief accountant.

"I'm talking about one in particular," Herbie replied. He shook his head and went on, "Could you believe that somebody at the top could make a mistake and, apparently to save face, let the error go down through planning, tooling, estimating and production not only to the point where metal was cut but to the major sub-assembly stage? Could you also believe that the sub-assemblies concerned, which in one case had been intended for the Panda module if they had been properly dimensioned, did not reach the scrap pile? They were dumped somewhere out of sight for a while and eventually sold or written off in such a way that on paper, at least, we did not show a loss."

"Incredible . . . " said Carson.

By the time he left Patterson's office he was in possession of a great deal of information on clerical trace-covering but knew very little about what it was that was being covered up. He had done about as much prying as it was possible for him to do into Reg Saunderson's department without making his interest too obvious, but there was the module final assembly and inspection area which was the joint responsibility of the project members Brady and Soames. He had time to get there with a few minutes to spare before lunch.

George Long was a big, soft-spoken man who smiled a lot, but it put an unfair strain on his good humor when someone like Carson started a complicated and seemingly pointless conversation with him just a few minutes before lunch break.

The timing had been deliberate, however. Carson did not want to give the impression that he was interested in anything in particular, and he had a theory that a man in a hurry somewhere told more and remembered less than one with plenty of time to talk.

"This is not a security matter, George, but I worry about it sometimes," said Carson, worriedly. "The stuff is scrap —very expensive scrap, I admit—but of little or no value to the company. At the same time it would be wrong for people to take it home . . . "

"I take your point, Joe," said George, shaking his head in awe. "Gawd, just imagine a rabbit hutch made from part of a Panda nose-cone! That really would be getting one up on the neighbors. But don't worry yourself about it. We are forced to reject components, even major sub-assemblies, for various reasons and they are either modified or scrapped. But we do not allow the men to take them away. As a matter of fact, in some cases we don't even sell them to the scrap metal dealers. I don't know what happens to them ultimately, but I believe some of them can be used for structural testing or for ground training purposes . . . "

"George," said Carson suddenly. "Don't let me keep you late for lunch . . . "

The end-of-shift siren was not loud enough to drown the hypothetical sound of another piece of the puzzle falling into place.

During lunch Carson thought that it was a ridiculous way to carry out an investigation. His only consolation was that the people engaged on this project-that-never-was had to be similarly circumspect in everything they did and said. They had to be especially careful how they used people, people like Pebbles. Was it possible that his promotion to the HE93 test program had been planned by the project members because they had in mind a more important use for him than moving waste paper? The HE93 was not sensitive, of course, but once into a structural test area it was very much easier to move across ladders of promotion than it was to move up. He would not have

35

minded betting that Pebbles would apply for another transfer in the not too distant future.

He would have to find out a lot more about the man. It was a good thing that he had good, acceptable reasons—as well as the real ones—for the questions he was going to ask Dr. Marshall.

Like Herbie Patterson, Dr. Marshall also felt indebted to Carson—although in her case the parking slot was forty yards from her office and it had been given to her simply because, in Carson's opinion, she was the best-looking girl in the company . . .

As assistant to the company medical officer, Dr. Marshall had a small, neat office which was almost filled by a well-worn desk, filing cabinets, bookshelves and framed diplomas. She was responsible for a good deal of the medical department's administration as well as performing the usual medical duties. An air of spaciousness was given the tiny room by the single glass wall which looked down across the cubicles, examination tables and fittings of the main treatment room. A casualty was having some foreign body washed out of his eye by one of the nurses, so it looked as if he would be able to talk to the doctor without fear of interruption.

"Good afternoon, Doctor," said Carson. "I wonder if you can help me."

She gave him a brief, intent, wholly professional look, then seeing no indications of physical or mental distress, she relaxed and said, "If I can, Mr. Carson. Please sit down."

"Thank you," said Carson. "I'm trying to find out as much as I can about a man called Pebbles."

It was obvious that she was not too happy about this one, even if she did feel obliged to him.

"I don't want you to betray a medical confidence or anything like that," Carson went on. "This is not idle curiosity. You may have heard about a small fire we had a few days ago. Someone—perhaps as a joke—used Mr. Pebbles to transport the combustibles to the site of the fire. As you probably know he is a very impressionable type,

36

easily led but not, so far as I could judge from only a few minutes' conversation with him, a moron.

"If I knew something about his background," Carson concluded, "I might be able to stop people making use of him like this."

"In that case," she said, smiling. "I don't mind discussing him with you. Physically he is A-1—no sick leave since he joined us, no industrial accidents or injuries. Since the pre-employment medical we haven't seen him here. I'm afraid there isn't much to tell."

Carson nodded. "Nevertheless I can't help feeling impressed by the way you reel off his medical history—or lack of it—without reference to the records. Can you do that with all twelve thousand of us, Doctor?"

Marshall laughed. "Only the memorable ones."

Carson said seriously. "I'm more interested in his mental condition. Bill Savage showed me his dossier, but it said nothing beyond the fact that he was retarded and classified as disabled. It did not go into his handicap in detail, and I'll need to know about that if I'm to talk to him without making him nervous and stop people playing dangerous jokes on him.

"Would you mind," he added, "telling me everything you can remember about the behavior of this memorable employee?"

She did not reply at once. Looking at her Carson thought that she was one of the most vital and attractive girls he had ever seen. Her wonderful complexion and skin was probably the result of her being light on cosmetics and heavy on the soap and water and not, as Carson had once believed as a very young man, because the things female doctors and nurses had to do caused a permanent blush. He wondered why she had not been married years ago, and whether she was really the iceberg everyone said she was or was she simply too dedicated to her profession?

Were the face and splendid figure that even a doctor's shapeless white coat could not hide simply the result of good engineering and intelligence? A healthy, intelligent girl was usually good looking—the healthy body *had* to be

37

well-proportioned and it was intelligence which lit up the face . . .

Which brought him back to Pebbles who was, it seemed, only physically perfect.

"I wasn't present at his pre-employment physical, you understand," she said suddenly. "My only direct contact with him was while I was administering the visual acuity tests."

Considering the man's disability and the job he was intended to fill, the tests had been a formality. If he could have distinguished the outline of the chart, he was through! But it was obvious from the start that the test was worrying Pebbles. He had looked confused and frightened and oddly helpless. He had stammered and sweated and could not even make an attempt at reading the chart. At one point she had been afraid that he would break down and cry.

She had explained to him that it was only necessary to read the first three lines. She pointed to the three lines he had to read and then she had left him alone in the room for a few minutes, expecting that he would cheat by moving closer and memorizing the lines she had indicated. But when she had returned he was still staring at the chart, moving his lips and looking puzzled. She thought that nobody could be that stupid but she wanted to be sure.

It was rather like trying to draw out a shy and emotionally disturbed child—she already had had some experience in that area—except that the child was six feet tall and built like Tarzan.

His trouble, it had gradually become clear, stemmed from the fact he was only just learning to read. Proudly he had shown her a magazine he had in his hip pocket. It was the first part of a children's encyclopedia of the type published in a series of weekly installments. There was a big, garish letter "A" on the cover surrounded by pictures of animals, amphibians, airplanes, astronomical telescopes and so on. The interior illustrations were very simple and the type-face large and open. Pebbles had said that the doctor at the clinic had given him the book when he had left to come to the aircraft factory. He had shown her the three pictures of different kinds of airplanes in the book and the fifty or so short, simple words describing what they were and how they worked, and he told her proudly that he had been studying the book to help him do his job better when he started work here. The reason he could not read the chart was because the letters on the chart were made differently.

He had asked if it would be all right if he drew pictures of the letters he could see. She had said yes and handed him a pencil and scratch pad . . .

" . . . It took a long time," she concluded in the tone of one not expecting to be believed, "but he copied down every blasted letter on the chart, *right down to the last line!*"

She stopped, but it was obvious that she wanted to say much more. Carson nodded and said quietly, "So he had perfect eyesight as well as muscles. But how did he impress you as a person?"

"He made me furious!" she said, her healthy color deepening with remembered emotion. "There he stood, as perfect a physical specimen as I'm ever likely to see, but looking at me the way a kid looks at the teacher on his first day at school! He was so childish, so . . . so innocent . . . I wanted to spit or maybe burst into tears at the injustice of it all." She tried, not very successfully, to laugh. "Of course, professional etiquette forbade my doing either."

"Of course."

"As a fairly normal, healthy, twenty-eight-year-old spinster of this parish," she went on, still trying not to be serious, "I have had usual maternal and other instincts. Seeing him standing there, he was such a baby as well as being a man—it hit me a double wallop above *and* below the belt, if you know what I mean. All I can say is that when that overgrown baby reaches the age, if he ever does, of taking an interest in girls, he'll be irresistible and I'll envy every single one of them!"

She took a deep breath, then ended. "That is how Mr. Pebbles impressed me, Mr. Carson. I have the qualifications to undertake an even deeper and more searching self-analysis, but probably I've shocked you enough for one day. Do you want to talk to my chief about this?"

Carson shook his head and stood up. "You've been very helpful, Doctor, thank you. Well, I'll be seeing you."

She looked up at him—not very far up because she was a tall girl—and he had the uncomfortable feeling that he was being analyzed now. Suddenly she smiled and said, "I doubt that, Mr. Carson. You're like John Pebbles, you never take sick . . . "

Chapter 7

That night Carson worked later than usual. He was spending so much time on his unofficial inquiries that burning the midnight fluorescents was the only way he could move the routine paperwork which was piling up. But tonight his mind refused to stay permanently in focus even on the simple jobs. It kept wandering, always in the same direction.

While processing parking space applications he found himself wondering if Pebbles could drive. If he had ever applied for a parking slot, that would be the obvious way of making friends with him by putting him under an obligation . . .

Meanwhile, Bill Savage had sent him an urgent memo. His problem was that several department heads were crying out for staff. The staff in question had been interviewed and accepted, their starting notices were ready and waiting to go out to them, but they had not yet been cleared by Security. Bill would be most grateful if the matter could be expedited.

There was very little Carson could do about that one. Security clearance of new employees—unless they were starting fairly high on the ladder—was simply a matter of checking nationality, place of birth, nationality of parents and relatives, political activities and police record, if any,

41

and seeing whether the person concerned traveled a lot or had spent a good part of his life in another country. The local police did most of the work and all too often they, with their quota of villains to catch, had ideas regarding the priorities which were not shared by Bill Savage.

It occurred to Carson that he should check on Pebbles' clearance. For several seconds he dithered between doing it there and then or leaving it until Monday, but the top-heavy aspect of his IN tray kept him in his seat.

There was an unusually large number of reclassifications in the pile. Hart-Ewing had no Top Secret projects going —not officially, that was—but there were a few hoary old Secrets and Restricteds connected with the HE93 missile guidance system which had been fighting a losing battle with the more speculative technical journals for several months. These had finally been declassified and they included technical material and strike photographs which Simpson had recently been seeking permission to publish.

It might be an idea to deliver the good news in person. Simpson would appreciate that. As well, the publicity man was fond of saying that it was his job to know everything so that he would know what *not* to write about. Simpson was also responsible for editing the house magazine, whose correspondents sent in news and gossip from every corner of Hart-Ewing. Without being aware of it Simpson might have some useful information about the project-without-a-name, and Pebbles.

Carson yawned, stretched and looked at his watch. In a few minutes it would be Saturday morning and he really should go to bed before he went to sleep. But before he locked up he had another quick look at the contents of the old envelope at the bottom of his junk drawer. It offended his orderly mind that the project he was trying to uncover did not, so far as he knew, have a name. It was easier to think about something which had a clear label attached to it, even if it was the wrong label in the beginning. One could not think constructively about nothing.

Project Hush? Triple-Hush? Firebug? Blank? Zero? *Remérant?* Yehudi . . . ?

They were ridiculous labels, not worth considering—but there had been precedents for ridiculous project names even at Hart-Ewing. Shortly after Carson had joined the company a man-portable missile project called Peashooter had been declassified and a more dignified appellation had been sought, in vain. The engineers responsible for R and D could think of no other name for the weapon system, the Government and military authorities concerned with financing and field trials insisted that a change of name would cause needless confusion in their paperwork, and the result had been that the Hart-Ewing ad-men had been given the job of making Peashooter sound like the supersonic Wrath of God . . .

Which made him think of the unfairly handicapped Pebbles again. His mental development had not been completely retarded because he was able, in his own simple fashion, to plan ahead and learn. Carson had a mental picture of him standing stripped to the waist, clutching a children's encyclopedia giving basic information about airplanes because he was joining an aircraft company.

Then there was Pebbles' tie.

Was it another try at preparing himself for the job? If so, had the tie helped him any more than the encyclopedia to sweep floors? Carson felt sure now that the other's transfer and promotion had not been gained on his own merits. The kids' book had not helped and he could just as well have used the tie, or any tie, to hold up his pants. Weather permitting, he would check on the tie business this weekend, but in the meantime he should try to think of something different and pleasant or he would end up dreaming about the man all night.

The first really pleasant subject to occur to him was Doctor Marshall and he kept a close mental hold on it, wishing that the hold was even closer and physical, on the way to his flat. But even then Pebbles kept creeping in, looking wide-eyed, innocent, and without his shirt on . . .

It rained all day Saturday but Sunday morning looked promising. Carson, with a drive of seventy-odd miles ahead of him, set out shortly before eleven-thirty, intend-

43

ing to have lunch at the clubhouse. The thought of having lunch out was pleasant—he would not have to cook it himself and, even if he would be unable to read or have his hi-fi blasting, neither would he have to do the washing up.

Carson had not been aware until then of just how discontented he was becoming. He was no psychologist, but even he knew that preferring a round trip of one hundred and fifty miles to making his own lunch was indicative of something seriously wrong somewhere. His depression was not being helped by the weather. A warm front was going through earlier than had been forecast and he was driving into a thickening overcast, and by the time he reached the club, visibility was down to two miles, the windsock hung like a limp yellow rag, and the cloud-base was down to six hundred feet and weeping steadily.

He called first at the Tower, a brightly painted hut towering all of nine feet. It was occupied by a young man wearing glasses and talking on the telephone. He nodded, raised the level of his voice to include Carson, and went on. " . . . The Met office says the wind will probably freshen late this afternoon, so this muck will be with us for another five hours at least. I don't think it is worth your while driving down today, Mr. Collins, unless you leave it until a couple of hours before dusk. No. Yes, definitely. I'm sorry, too—I was booked for a cross-country to . . . Fine, I'll do that. G'bye."

To Carson he said, "You heard that, friend. No flying this afternoon. But if you're looking for the CFI he's in the bar. *Everybody's* in the bar."

"Actually I'm looking for Mr. Pebbles," said Carson. "Is he here today?"

"Really? Not so far. But if you should see Bob Chambers in there, will you remind him, not too politely, that he was supposed to relieve me twenty minutes ago?"

The bar occupied one side of a large room whose walls were covered with pictures of airplanes, flight safety posters and beer advertisements. There was a one-armed bandit standing in a corner, a TV which was not yet

44

switched on—the weather had not yet driven them to utter desperation—and a large number of leather armchairs which time and hard usage had rendered form-fitting. As Carson entered someone, probably the tardy Bob Chambers, hurried out. Everybody, he saw at a glance, comprised twelve people.

They were standing at the bar in groups of twos and threes. One of the groups comprised Maxwell, the club's chief flying instructor, another man Carson did not know and . . . Wayne Tillotson. Carson walked through to the dining room to organize his thoughts and to order lunch.

The second was easy but the first was made virtually impossible by the arrival of the man he had already met in the tower, whose duties apparently included those of honorary PRO.

"My psychiatrist worries if I talk to myself," he said cheerfully. "Do you mind if I sit with you? Thanks. I'm Jeff Donnelly. We . . . " He hesitated delicately, glanced at Carson's tie, then finished, " . . . haven't seen you around recently."

"Joe Carson," said Carson, putting down his knife to shake hands. "You haven't seen me around for about six years. I'm afraid my membership has well and truly lapsed and, until I can find your current Treasurer, I'm wearing this quiet but distinguished neck-piece under false pretenses. You see, when I first joined it was late summer and all your instructors were fully booked. I did mean to try again later, but other things kept cropping up . . . "

The truth was that he had just joined Hart-Ewing and he had thought, erroneously, that a little knowledge of flying would be useful in his new job. Looking back, there had not been all that much difference between Pebbles and himself . . .

"You've found him," said Donnelly, laughing. "Welcome back, and don't bother paying me until after dessert—I don't want to give the impression that I'm rushing you or that the club is short of funds. Do you know any of the other members?"

"Well . . ." began Carson.

"I'll introduce you around. And don't worry if you appear to be ignored at first. Their minds are usually on something else—beer, girls, sometimes even flying—and your presence will eventually register. What do you do in real life?"

"I'm security officer at Hart-Ewing."

"Is that so? I personally would have expected something more obnoxious, with jutting jaws and suspicious steely eyes. Anyway, you'll see lots of Hart-Ewing faces around here—you probably saw Wayne Tillotson already. And if you're wondering why he belongs to a flying club like this, he'll tell you that flying fifty tons of computer makes him lose touch with reality and removes his brain an uncomfortable distance from the seat of his pants.

"Of course," Jeff Donnelly went on cheerfully, "Tillotson *trusts* the seat of his pants. I couldn't trust mine if it was sitting on a stack of Bibles—my instrument flying is atrocious . . ." He broke off, waved and called, "Bob, over here!"

Tillotson and Maxwell, who had been about to sit down at another table, turned and came towards them. Carson swore under his breath. Tillotson's presence had come as an unpleasant surprise and he needed time to decide on an approach which would not make the chief test pilot suspicious.

If only the well-meaning Donnelly would not mention that he had asked about Pebbles . . .

". . . Really be a fatted calf instead of cold ham salad," Donnelly was saying. "After a six-year pause for reconsideration, Joe has decided to learn to fly one of these newfangled heavier-than-air machines. And he has asked for John Peebles, too . . ."

You, thought Carson helplessly, *and your big mouth!*

"Really?" said the instructor, looking mildly surprised. He was the kind of quiet, deliberate and imperturbable person who would react mildly to the crack of doom. He went on, "John will be very pleased about that. Not many people do, you know. He's good and we all like him, but

46

a certain amount of caution is to be expected, wouldn't you say?"

Carson had the panicky feeling that he had missed something even though he had heard every word the other had said. What was Pebbles here? He was good at his job, but people were wary of him. Was he a combination club mascot and village idiot? Were they sorry for him and tolerated him for laughs? Did he sweep the floor or maybe do odd jobs in the hangar, just for the privilege of being close to airplanes and pilots? Did some soft-hearted flyer sometimes take him up for a flight? Carson did not know but, because he had asked for Pebbles, he was expected to know.

Know *what?*

When in doubt, he thought desperately, say something so obviously ridiculous that it can only be a joke instead of a display of ignorance. While they were laughing he might gain some idea of what it was he was supposed to have said . . .

"Does Pebbles do much solo flying these days?"

Nobody laughed.

Maxwell was mildly serious rather than mildly amused as he said, "Mr. Carson, we don't pay our weekend instructors for flying solo."

Chapter 8

The sun came out for keeps just a few minutes after six o'clock and Pebbles arrived at six-ten. He was the same shy, awkward man Carson had met a few days earlier, but the difference became apparent as soon as he began to talk. In these surroundings he had a sort of diffident, but very real, authority.

As they walked out to the aircraft he called Carson "Mr. Carson" and, with some vague idea that the other's confidence needed boosting and to show that outside of working hours they were equals, Carson called him "Mr. Pebbles." As a result the conversation was painfully formal.

Carson's introduction to G-ARTZ was equally formal. Pebbles walked around the aircraft, explaining the necessity for checking for external damage which might have been sustained to the prop, flying surfaces, landing gear and tires since the last flight check. Then he looked at Carson with the anxious air of a father watching his favorite daughter go off with a boy friend of dubious character, and finally indicated the wing walkway and the open cockpit canopy.

"B-before you strap in, Mr. Carson," he said, "You'll f-feel much better without your jacket . . ."

Despite the bright sunshine, the wind blowing across the

wet airfield cut like a knife. Carson took off his jacket as suggested and placed it behind his seat, noting as he did so that Pebbles kept his jacket on, wondering which of them was mentally retarded.

Carson had not come to the club with the intention of taking a flying lesson, and certainly not from Pebbles, but somehow he had worked himself into the position of not being able to avoid it.

"At H-Hart-Ewing's," began Pebbles diffidently, "you will have picked up a f-fair knowledge of flying theory . . ."

There followed a shy but persistent inquisition which proved, much to Carson's own surprise, that he did in fact know about dihedral, incidence, angles of attack, effect of controls and the theory of flight generally. Then Pebbles leaned across and strapped him in very firmly.

Carson fought the urge to hit the quick-release buckle and run.

"B-before starting the engine," said Pebbles, "there are a number of checks to be carried out. I'll tell you what they are as I do them. D-don't worry if you can't remember everything the first few times, it will come . . ." As he continued talking, pointing and switching-on, Carson became firmly convinced that he would not be able to remember *anything*. Then Pebbles, his stammer completely gone, was saying ". . . Look around carefully to see that the area is clear and that your slipstream will not inconvenience anyone, then pull this starter and release it when the engine fires.

"Pull the starter, Mr. Carson . . ."

Carson did as he was told, thinking cynically that he was being conned into feeling that he was making a contribution, however small, to what was going on. It was probably club policy designed to make the student pilot feel less like shooting himself through sheer inadequacy. The funny thing was that it worked, even though he knew he was being had . . .

"Before taxi-ing there is a second series of checks which include testing the flying controls. Today you can go through them with me . . ." Pebbles began, and about five

49

minutes later ended, ". . . Have another good lookout for people, objects or other aircraft taxi-ing in the vicinity, then release the brakes and open the throttle enough to overcome the aircraft's inertia, and move off at a fast walking pace.

"Look around," Pebbles said clearly over the sound of the engine, "release the brake and open the throttle, Mr. Carson . . ."

G-ARTZ lurched forward and rocked across the grass in the general direction of the taxiway. Carson began to sweat. The great unwieldy brute was rolling over the grass out of control, the engine noise made it hard to think and Pebbles was an out-and-out nutcase to allow Carson to risk an expensive airplane like this.

" . . . You are moving too fast, Mr. Carson," Pebbles was saying. "This exaggerates the effect of the nose-wheel steering. Throttle back. More. A fast walking pace, remember? When we come to the edge of the taxiway you will have to turn and travel along it to the end of the runway. Before you turn, throttle back and use the brake to bring us almost to a stop, otherwise you will strain the landing gear, which is not stressed to take heavy side loadings.

"Close the throttle. That's it. Brake . . . "

They rolled onto the tarmac and came almost to a stop before Carson pressed hard against the rudder bar. G-ARTZ swung around and he straightened the nose-wheel, opened the throttle and began wobbling along the taxiway at the required fast walking pace. It was slightly easier to control the thing on a paved surface than it had been on grass—very slightly easier, and "control" was hardly the word.

His shirt was sticking to his back, his tie was strangling him, and the cockpit felt like a turkish bath.

" . . . Try to keep in the center of the taxiway, Mr. Carson," said the voice in his right ear, "and remember that your wings project nearly fifteen feet on each side. Don't pass too close to that fuel bowser. That's good. You

50

concentrate on the aircraft and I'll handle the radio this time . . ."

Pebbles unclipped the mike, brought it to within half an inch of his lips and said something which was lost in the noise of the engines. From the back of the cabin an over-amplified voice rattles, "You are clear to the holding point on runway Zero Nine, Tango Zulu. Acknowledge please."

Pebbles' lips moved again, then he racked the mike and said, "The holding point is that white line about fifty yards ahead. As you come up to it, close the throttle, brake and swing the aircraft until it is pointing downwind at an angle of forty-five degrees to the runway, then lock the brakes. You will then be in a position to see if the runway is clear and that there are no aircraft making their final approach. If there is an aircraft on finals, your attitude will tell him that you are waiting for him to land . . .

"That's good. Now *lock* the brakes, Mr. Carson. We perform our pre-takeoff checks at this point. There is a simple mnemonic which will help you remember the sequence, but this time just do it with me. Trim, set. Throttle, set to fast tickover and friction nut not too tight. Mixture, rich. Carburetor, cold . . ."

He can do multiplication and division, Carson thought crazily, *and joined-up handwriting and . . .* But there was no time to think about that. He could not remember a time in his whole life when he had felt so harassed and frightened and excited. Pebbles was a blithering idiot to expect . . .

But then Pebbles was supposed to be an idiot, so simple-minded that he might very well think that six years in an aircraft factory had given Carson a greater understanding of airplanes than Pebbles had gained in three. It was possible that Pebbles' mind worked like that.

The sweat running from Carson's pores changed from hot to cold.

"Tango Zulu," roared the voice from the back, "you are clear for takeoff." Pebbles added, "Release the brake,

51

Mr. Carson, open the throttle and move into the center of the runway. Line up the nose with that clump of trees on the skyline—that's a useful landmark during takeoffs from zero nine, especially if there is a crosswind trying to blow you off course. No, we are not quite centered, but it wasn't bad for a first try . . ."

Carson blinked sweat out of his eyes and croaked something which was unintelligible even to himself.

"I'll handle the takeoff, if you don't mind. But keep your feet lightly on the rudder pedals, your right hand on the control column and your left on the throttle—I want you to get the feel of things for next time. Right? I have control . . ."

"The words have not been invented," said Carson fervently, "to properly express my relief."

Pebbles nodded seriously and opened the duplicate throttle. The engine roared and they surged forward, picking up speed by the second. Under his feet the pedals made small, almost unnoticeable movements, keeping them centered on the runway, and Pebbles was talking about watching the ASI for the unstick speed. The control column moved back a fraction of an inch, the undercarriage stopped rumbling against the ground, and they were airborne. The runway dropped away, the clubhouse and the diminutive control tower slid under the edge of the port wing. The heads of the people standing outside it were exactly the same size as the wing rivets.

There were things he was supposed to do and remember at three hundred feet and six hundred feet and a thousand feet and Pebbles was telling him about them in detail, but Carson was watching the cars on the main road and Tango Zulu's shadow flickering across them.

"Sorry," he said. "I was enjoying the view."

"You aren't supposed to enjoy the view in the early lessons," said Pebbles. "If you'll look at the airspeed indicator, altimeter, engine rev counter and the attitude of the airplane at the moment, you will see that our speed is seventy knots and that we are climbing under full power. I want you to maintain this attitude by judging the position of the horizon in the windscreen and watching the ASI. If the needle falls below seventy it means we are climbing too steeply and may stall—there is an audible warning before this point is reached—unless the climb angle is reduced. Should the speed increase, this means the climbing angle has flattened and we are not gaining height at the optimum rate.

"To decrease the angle of climb," he went on, "ease the control column very gently forward. To increase the climb, ease it back. If one wing drops, correct by moving the stick to the opposite side. Very small movements of the control column are sufficient. Do you understand, Mr. Carson?"

Carson nodded.

"When the altimeter shows fifteen hundred feet, ease the stick forward to level out," said Pebbles. "Then close the throttle until the engine rev counter shows 22,000 r.p.m. That is an economical cruising power for level flight. You have control."

Carson began to perspire again, freely. The nose started to drop and he eased the stick back. Immediately Tango Zulu tried to stand on its tail and the stall warning beeped querulously. He pushed the stick slightly forward and they arced over into a dive. One wing went down and he compensated for that, then the other wing dropped and he over-compensated for *that*. The horizon was sliding about all over the place and the aircraft seemed to be in a continuous three-dimensional skid that he had no hope of controlling . . .

"This is a very responsive airplane," said Pebbles as he put a steadying hand on the control column. "Relax, Mr. Carson. Right? You have control."

It was like trying to balance on a single stilt. Carson gritted his teeth and labored furiously at not moving anything more than a fraction of an inch in any direction. When he levelled out at fifteen hundred feet, throttled back to cruising power and held the thing in fairly straight and more or less level flight, he thought he deserved more than five minutes watchful silence followed by directions for making a gentle turn to starboard . . .

He made several gentle turns to port and starboard. He had the odd sensation of being motionless while pictures of the hazy blue sky, the horizon and the patchwork of roads and fields below were flat images projected onto the outside of the perspex canopy. To move the pictures in a way that would please Pebbles, one had to be very neat and accurate in one's movements. Carson tried very hard to do it neatly, the way he did most things, and gradually he began to think that his slipping and skidding all over the sky might not be just as bad as when he started.

More and more often he looked at the ground below while he was banking, at the doll's houses, doll's villages and town, at the roads like black shoe-laces and the microscopic cars, asking himself what the hell he was doing up here? But the question was rhetorical.

He was flying an airplane.

His body felt as if it was being boiled in its own sweat. His shoulders and neck ached with tension and his teeth were clenched so tightly his jaw hurt. But suddenly he wanted to laugh, and did.

Pebbles said, "Head for the airfield, Mr. Carson. We don't want to work you too hard on the first day . . ."

He had wanted to talk to Pebbles, but the instructor had to take up another pupil as soon as they landed. Carson was not too disappointed, however—his feet had not yet touched the ground and he doubted his ability to hold any sort of coherent conversation with anyone. When Jeff Donnelly met him later in the clubhouse, it was a good thing that the treasurer did all the talking.

"How did you make out, Joe? Terrible, eh? All thumbs. One of the early fringe benefits of learning to fly is that you lose two pounds during every lesson. But don't worry, it will come.

"John works you hard, though," Jeff rattled on. "But then if you want to sightsee you should be in the passenger seat, right? He's a bit finicky about checks and inspections, too—treats Tango Zulu like a super-sonic jet, or as if he's married to it and they're still on their honeymoon! I'm not criticizing him, mind. If you learn to fly like John Pebbles you'll certainly die in bed . . ."

During the drive back Carson kept thinking how strange and pleasant it was to have a horizon which remained horizontal even when he came to a sharp bend. And later, when he was back at his flat, he found that he could not concentrate on a book, or listen to a record or do anything but sit watching the mental tele-recording which played itself over and over in his mind's eye. When he went to bed it was even worse.

Learning to fly had been something he had wanted to do as a kid, and now it was, or should be, simply a means of getting closer to Pebbles for security reasons. But his normal, everyday thought processes seemed to have suffered multiple derailment. He found it impossible to think coherently about the shy, stupid, Hart-Ewing Pebbles, or the ultra-secret project or anything but the ground and sky as they had looked from fifteen hundred feet, tilting and wheeling around him because he told them to. It was like asking a man to think about routine office work on his honeymoon.

Carson had never been on a honeymoon, but he felt that it was a true analogy.

Chapter 9

There had been a succession of fine weekends, so good that Carson had learned how to fly straight and level, climb, descend, perform gentle turns and survive the rather hectic lesson on stall recovery. On his third lesson he wobbled down the runway and staggered into the air with the stall warning hooting derisively all the way up to three hundred feet. It was possibly the worst takeoff ever perpetrated, but it had been all his own work.

Subsequent takeoffs improved and he moved on to circuits and landing. He would continue to do circuits and landings until he satisfied Pebbles and the CFI that he could take off *and* land safely. He had been sitting within a few inches of Pebbles for something like seven hours without being able to get really close to him.

"Does he make you feel uncomfortable, Joe?" said Jeff Donnelly when Carson brought up the subject during lunch. "You can change your instructor if you like. Have a word with the CFI."

"I'm not uncomfortable with him," said Carson, then added, "Well, perhaps a little, when he's expecting me to land that thing and the runway won't hold still. I don't want to change instructors, but outside flying time he seems to avoid me—or is it just my inferiority complex showing?"

"No," said Jeff seriously. "He is a first-class pilot and instructor, but some people remember him as he used to be and talk about it to newcomers when they ought to know better. We like him and—"

"If you don't let me in on this dark and desperate secret," said Carson, "I shall die of a curable disease, curiosity!"

"That," said Donnelly, "is one of the sneakiest forms of blackmail I have ever encountered . . ."

According to Donnelly, Pebbles had been coming to the club for about three years—four or five months, in fact, before he had joined Hart-Ewing. He had come to their attention first as an odd, rather pathetic character who daily haunted the edge of the airfield in the morning and afternoon to watch the planes take off and land.

When he began wandering into the hangar for a closer look at the aircraft, they had tried to shoo him away, but gently because he looked so desperately puzzled about everything they said to him and his clothes were always muddy and rumpled. Then one day he arrived looking as if he had fallen into a muddy ditch and somebody had taken him into the clubhouse to dry off. They discovered that he was not a tramp, that except for the fresh mud his clothes were clean and that he was not a nut— just retarded, childish.

So they found odd jobs for him to do. He could not talk very well and some of the mistakes he made in word and deed were very . . . elementary. When he was not tidying the clubhouse or helping make sandwiches behind the bar, he could always be found standing beside a plane and looking into the cockpit, his face like that of a child trying to do a difficult problem in mental arithmetic.

On the week end of the yearly international rally, when aircraft from all over had flown in to take part in the first day's flying display, John Pebbles had turned up in a dark suit with only his shoes muddy and no tie. The CFI's wife had insisted that Jeff Donnelly give him a club tie—he had learned how to clean his shoes by then—because he never took the money they tried to give him from time to

57

time. He did not seem to understand money, nor was he capable of using public transport to get from where he lived to the airfield, hence the muddy shoes. Somehow he had become the club mascot, replacing the export reject cross-eyed idol somebody had brought back from India, and without being too forceful about it the members let it be known that this was one lame dog who was not to be kicked.

Two weeks after the rally Wayne Tillotson visited the club to get, as he was fond of putting it, the taste of flying supersonic computers out of his mouth. On impulse he had taken John Pebbles in the passenger seat and, being a cautious man, strapped him in very firmly in case their mascot got violent. But the precaution was unnecessary—Pebbles' reaction, according to Tillotson, had been one of excitement approaching ecstasy. Again on impulse he had allowed Pebbles to take control.

They were gone for over two hours and when they returned Tillotson would not talk about the trip in detail. Pebbles had tried to say a lot but he did not at that time have the vocabulary and he was so excited that he stuttered like a machine-gun. Shortly afterwards Tillotson got him a job in Hart-Ewing.

It was not a very good or well-paid job, Donnelly understood, but Pebbles did not smoke or drink or have girl friends, so he had been able to spend most of his pay on flying lessons. He qualified very quickly and stopped being the club mascot, although if anything the members liked him even more and were intensely proud of him for the way he had overcome his disability. Later he got his instructor's rating, which allowed him to fly more while actually being paid a small fee for doing so, and he had checked out on several twin-engined types and was talking of trying for his commercial licence.

Flying, studying and working at Hart-Ewing was all that he seemed to do. Apparently he was trying to broaden his studies as much as possible, but he still dropped conversational bricks and made elementary, but embarrassing, mistakes on social occasions.

When they heard about his background, newcomers to the club sometimes worried about the possibility of his having a mental relapse while flying with them ...

"... I'm no psychologist," Jeff went on quickly, "but he seems to be improving mentally rather than falling back. We all thought he was retarded at first—you know, a grown man with the mind of a child. In many ways he still is a child, but not in an airplane! I wish I knew what went wrong with him as a kid, Joe. It's as if his intelligence was there all the time, building up pressure, just waiting for someone to pull the plug out.

"More than anyone else," Donnelly ended seriously, "it was Tillotson who pulled out the plug. Pebbles has never looked back since then."

"This," said Carson, "is an unbelievable story. But I believe you."

"Gee, thanks."

"... In fact," Carson went on, "it is remarkably like a wish-fulfillment dream. You know, boy watches planes taking off and landing, gets the chance of a flight, finds he is a natural-born pilot, qualifies for more complex aircraft, culminating in him becoming a top test pilot and being considered for inclusion in the next batch of trainee astronauts ..."

Astronauts, he thought; *Tau Ceti* ...

"... But pilots are not born, they are made," Carson continued. "In my case with extreme difficulty. It's rather disquieting to think that someone who doesn't know enough about money to ride on a bus is teaching me to fly ..."

A shade apprehensively, Donnelly said, "I didn't mean to worry you, Joe. He has come a long way since—"

"Relax," said Carson. "I told you that I don't intend changing my instructor at this stage. Besides, if we are all figments of John Pebbles' wish-fulfillment dream, I don't think I would be able to ..."

On the way home he drove past Pebbles' address and stopped at the police station two streets farther on. He knew the station inspector from 'way back and should,

59

by pulling the old pals act, be able to keep his inquiries unofficial even though they had never liked each other when they had worked together. George Russell had been big, loud, sarcastic and insensitive in those days and apparently only his voice had changed for the better.

"Pebbles isn't exactly a public enemy," said Inspector Russell quietly. "He broke a window once playing ball in the street with kids less than half his age and size, but he paid for it. Are you chasing spies again, Joe?"

"No, George," said Carson, and explained, "he is a dimwit about some things and there is danger of him getting into serious trouble at the factory because he is so easily led. I need a little background information about his home life and so on—to help me understand him before I start talking to him like a very stern father."

"You always were a lousy policeman, Joe, and you haven't changed a bit," said Russell, laughing. "With crime —the detection of criminals—you were very good indeed. But punishment—especially the punishment of habitual or petty criminals—always seemed to bother you. I suppose that was why you resigned from the force . . ."

"That was it," said Carson drily. "There weren't enough master criminals to keep me occupied. But about Pebbles . . .?"

Russell laughed again. "I didn't think you needed to check on mental defectives—oh, all right, I'm just pulling your leg. He boards with a widow called Kirk. Well, not exactly a widow—her husband left her shortly after their first child, a mongol boy, was born and hasn't been seen since. She really loved that boy, even though there were complications which meant that he couldn't live much past nine or ten years. When he died about four years ago she went to pieces for a while, until Pebbles came along. Now she treats him as her son, is intensely proud of the way he is improving, going to night school and so on. I think she tells herself that if her own boy had lived he might have been able to make good just like Pebbles has done.

"She's not quite right in the head," Russell concluded,

60

"but harmless and well-liked. Don't worry her with this, Joe."

"I won't even have to talk to her," said Carson as he rose to go. He could not help adding, "You have changed quite a lot, George . . ."

Any real information about Pebbles' background would probably entail asking personal questions of the man himself. Perhaps if he tried to talk to him at Hart-Ewing instead of at the club, showed a friendly interest in his new job, something might develop. Among the test gantries and aircraft sections undergoing their continuing series of simulated takeoffs, wind-buffetings, engine vibration and landing shocks there would be no problems about which knife or spoon to use or how to keep food on the plate while eating.

But Pebbles was not available for questioning or as an object of friendly interest. Charlie Desmond, his new department head, said that he was owed two weeks' leave and had decided to take it before settling into the new job. Carson suggested that, while he was there, it might be a good idea to check door and window fastenings and the department's fire-fighting arrangements. Charlie said to be his guest and delegated Bob Menzies, one of his engineers, to go around with him.

While they were speaking the constant thump of simulated loads hitting wing and undercarriage specimens under test punctuated every word, hurrying on the conversation and doing nothing at all to soothe Carson's nerves or reduce his impatience. Pebbles' absence worried him for some reason and for reasons equally vague, he felt that the project was reaching a critical point. If only there was more information . . .

Menzies was not affected by the noises and talked easily and freely. About Pebbles he did not know anything for *sure*, but there were rumors that he was spending a working holiday doing a training course somewhere, probably as a preparation for his new job. Not for the clerical position in the HE93 test section, Menzies added—there was another rumor that when he returned Pebbles would

61

be moving again to a better job in the module test area.

A little later when Carson displayed mild interest—no one but himself knew the effort that mildness cost him—in the big, shining cone of a life support and command module which occupied a cradle in one of the storerooms, he was told that Menzies was not sure why it was there. The modules came in from time to time, they were defective and at a guess he would say that they were sold as scrap, or one of the Government agencies might have bought a few for training and simulation purposes.

But the best man to ask about that was Dreamy Daniels. The chief designer and his crowd were in the storeroom half the night, sometimes—measuring and fitting test equipment, Menzies supposed, to find out why such important hunks of hardware had to be rejected in the first place and to decide on a good story if one of themselves was responsible . . .

". . . I'm a cynic, Mr. Carson, if you haven't guessed that much already," Menzies said, laughing. "Oh, would you like to climb in? They even have a padded acceleration couch in this one . . ."

"Thank you," said Carson as he wriggled feet first into the hatch. He began to feel cynical, too, but for a different reason.

The couch was sinfully comfortable and, so far as he could see, complete with harness, air supplies and associated life support equipment. Facing him at waist level there was a control panel also complete except for one large, round hole which seemed to stare at him like a computer pirate through its empty eye socket. Through the opening there was enough light to show a space of perhaps four cubic feet and a bunch of cable looms, their individual strands opened and tagged where they were supposed to join the missing piece of equipment. Everything else in the module looked bright and new and complete, lacking only power to be fully functioning.

It had become impossible for him to believe that an intricate and expensive fabrication like this could reach

62

such an advanced stage before someone discovered an error which necessitated its being scrapped.

But if this vehicle was not to be scrapped, then it had to be the end-result of the secret project, or perhaps the equipment destined for that empty space was what the project was all about. At the same time the vehicle was small, almost as small as the early Mercury capsules. Did its size suggest that the Government was giving it only limited support? Perhaps the idea was potentially valuable but too radical to warrant the cost of pushing a greater weight into space. Or the missing device might do the pushing itself and be very dangerous to the crew . . .

The memory of the two charred pieces of paper came back to him. They had mentioned interstellar distances—when up until now manned spaceflight had yet to go beyond the Moon—and psychological damage to lab animals, and had suggested the use of a human guinea-pig so that exact data on these psychological effects would be available. Carson found himself imagining that he was in space, the instrument panel no longer missing its eye and an enigmatic something behind the panel at Go. His mental picture of the panel and of the awesome glimpse of eternity through the port was so real and sharp that he was angry when Menzies tapped him on the shoulder.

"You've been in there for nearly twenty minutes, Mr. Carson," he said with just a trace of impatience. "You're nearly as bad as John Pebbles—he likes playing astronaut, too. Of course, don't we all . . .?"

"I'm sorry, Bob," said Carson. But he spent another few minutes in the capsule anyway, memorizing the drawing reference numbers on the support brackets which would hold the missing piece of equipment behind the control panel. Herbie Patterson would be able to tell him which factory they had come from and, by a process of clerical crosschecking, something about the gadget they had been designed to support.

Chapter 10

Herbie Patterson died late the following evening. Always a very thorough and tidy man, he managed to kill himself thoroughly but not with tidiness.

In the Admin building there was a central well with stairs running up to all five floors and an elevator housing covered with a protective grill occupying most of the well space. Apparently Herbie had climbed all five flights of stairs—a feat which would almost certainly have killed him anyway—and thrown himself over the chest-high handrail at the top. Because of the narrowness of unobstructed space in the well he had hit the housing grillwork and handrails several times on the way down, leaving a shoe on the stairs leading up from the third floor and finally striking, partly demolishing, and impaling himself on, the wreckage of an empty crate on the ground floor.

Donovan found him, phoned Carson and Dr. Kennedy, then spent the time until their arrival keeping the few others who were working late that night from seeing too much of the body.

According to the senior patrol officer Mr. Patterson had passed him without speaking—which was very unusual—less than ten minutes before his fall. Donovan said that he did not look well. Carson had spoken to Herbie earlier that afternoon when he asked him to check on the capsule drawing reference numbers. Then he had been his usual, bitterly complaining self. Dr. Kennedy suggested that he might have learned suddenly of his heart condition and had decided to speed things up. Herbie never had much patience with inefficiency, in people, machinery or malfunctioning organs . . .

The incident put a three-day Hold on Carson's project inquiries while he tried vainly to get the picture of Herbie's shattered and bloody body out of his dreams. As well, Mrs. Patterson took her husband's death very hard even though she had been expecting him to go at any time, and their oldest child was only thirteen. But by the time the funeral arrangements were made and he had helped the widow straighten out her late husband's affairs, the project with all of its unresolved problems began to fill his mind once again.

But there were still no answers to the really important questions.

Sometimes he sat in his office and thought longingly of what he would do if only he could question these people, really question them with someone like George Russell looming over them as an unsettling influence while Carson asked leading questions. But he could not ask questions. Officially the subject he wished to discuss did not exist, and their security was really tight.

From the evidence he had been able to gather, it now seemed clear that the number of people aware of the project, as opposed to the thousands who were contributing to it in ignorance, was fairly small. Carson estimated their number at between twenty and thirty, placed strategically to deal with awkward questions regarding materials requisitions, design queries, pre-production planning, tooling, inspection and the ultimate disposal of the so-called scrapped sub-assemblies and assemblies. It had taken some really inspired thinking to devise and mount the operation in such a way that the necessary hardware was produced, developed and modified without anyone knowing what was really going on.

Dreamy Daniels was subject to long bouts of inspired thinking, otherwise he would not have been the design chief, but he was not the type to be bothered with finicky details like burning classified documentation, and neither were the other design people. The only other possibilities were that the project either carried its own security or had none at all. It was possible, but not at all likely, that Daniels had talked the authorities into supporting a major project without official security involvement by arguing that guards and highly classified paperwork drew attention to the thing they were trying to hide. But this did not explain the highly professional way in which they covered their traces. Someone who really knew his stuff was watching over them.

For some reason the thought of Herbie's shoe lying on the stairs below the third floor came into his mind—a soft, highly-polished black shoe with vertical scratches at the heel. The other shoe on Herbie's foot had been just like it, the scratching undoubtedly caused by his long tumble past the stair guard-rails and elevator housing. It was natural to assume that one shoe had been knocked off during the fall, and not lost while his unconscious body was being dragged up to the fifth floor from his ground floor office near the elevator. Nor was it unreasonable to think that the marks of the hypothetical blow which had knocked him unconscious had been concealed by the awful mess he had made of himself on the way down . . .

Angrily Carson gave himself a hard, mental shake. His impatience and frustration were making him dramatize things, making him try to bend *every* incident into evidence for the existence of the project.

Nevertheless, if Hart-Ewing had two security officers he would have to be even more careful in his inquiries. At the same time, secrets attracted spies like flies and the spy who penetrated this particular project would have to be very good indeed.

It would be a nice feather in his cap if it was Carson and not the shadow security officer who turned up a spy. But it was also worth bearing in mind the fact that if a project was sufficiently important anyone, even another security man insisting that he only wanted to help, taking an unauthorized interest in it would be immediately suspect. The top intelligence departments thought in devious, suspicious and sometimes ruthless ways, and Carson had no wish to be taken into a small, sound-proofed room somewhere and politely but firmly shot. The result was that he would have to either forget the whole thing or act more and more like the kind of spy he was hoping to uncover—if this very special spy existed in the first place!

John Pebbles came immediately to mind. He had arrived on the scene three years ago when, presumably, the project was getting under way and its future course was becoming clear. He had been brought into Hart-Ewing by one of the project personnel, Tillotson, and he had aided it by assisting—perhaps unknowingly—with the destruction of classified paperwork. Recently he had moved up in the world and was working—still possibly without being aware of it—on the project in a more important capacity. His outside activities were intriguing if not downright suspicious—people did not as a rule become pilots who, three years earlier, had not enough sense to come in out of the rain.

It was all very well to trot out the old adage about the best way to be inconspicuous was to be obvious. For a spy Pebbles was a shade *too* obvious. But if he was not a spy, could he be the shadow security officer? The facts could point equally strongly in that direction, and playing the character of an idiot gradually making good was an excellent cover.

The trouble was that Carson did not think Pebbles was playing any kind of part. Perhaps he was meant to think that because his emotions had been deliberately involved as part of the cover. But if Pebbles was acting then Carson wanted to opt out of the human race!

John Pebbles was being *used*, then. It had probably started with Tillotson feeling sorry for him and, knowing his fondness for airplanes, suggesting that he could sweep floors in the factory as easily as at the club. Now he was a project tool, a close examination of which should reveal some very useful information regarding the work it was meant to do.

A close examination . . .

Everything he knew about the man was secondhand except for his competence as a pilot. Carson could not now request a security re-check because that would undoubtedly arouse the suspicions of his opposite number. Neither could be inquire officially about Pebbles' previous addresses—because of his obvious low IQ at the time of employment, the original security check had been very sketchy indeed. All Carson could do was continue to gather secondhand information since that was the only kind available . . .

By suddenly deciding to run a check on the portable fire-fighting equipment in the apprentices' training section, he was able to chat with the instructors and boys about the night classes they attended in the local technical college. Although Carson was careful not to mention it, Pebbles' name cropped up several times, and he discovered that the other was farther advanced than any of the boys. He also discovered the name of one of Pebbles' teachers.

That evening he was able to arrange an accidental meeting with the teacher. He did not have to ask many questions—the man wanted to talk about Pebbles to anyone who would listen. John Pebbles was his star pupil, the sort of man he would like to have as a son, a sober, hardworking type of which there were far too few these days. As he talked it became obvious that he attributed part of Pebbles' academic success to his own teaching and methods of drawing the best out of a pupil who, in the beginning, had been a stumbling, near-wordless moron.

Looking at the enthusiastic, colorless, sickly little man Carson thought that Pebbles' phenomenal progress had helped an aging, disillusioned teacher as much as the teacher thought he had helped Pebbles.

Next day Carson sent for an ordnance survey map of the

68

flying club area. Before joining Hart-Ewing Pebbles had visited the flying club twice a day. Assuming that he had meals at the usual times and that he had gone home for them on foot, there was a certain maximum distance he had to travel even if he did walk straight across muddy fields instead of using the roads.

Carson allowed an hour for the midday meal, subtracted it from Pebbles' total time of absence from the airfield during the middle of the day and found that he was left with a traveling time in each direction of fifty minutes. He worked out the distance a man could walk in fifty minutes, added a little because Pebbles was enthusiastic and might have run part of the way, then with the airfield as the center drew a circle whose radius was the distance Pebbles had walked or run in fifty minutes.

The circle enclosed part of a small town, two farms and a very well-known institution. He looked at the tiny, fat L that was the hospital and thought *It is too ridiculously obvious to be true!*

In his pocket he had a letter from the club reminding him that he had to undergo a medical examination for his student pilot's license as soon as possible. It gave him the opportunity to practice a little delicate verbal probing once again on the delectable Dr. Marshall.

But it was Dr. Kennedy, an impossible man on whom to practice delicate verbal probing, who asked all the questions.

"Do you *have* to have your medical this morning? Don't you know I have a sales team going overseas, all wanting their shots this morning? Didn't Marshall tell you about the new intake of employees this morning? Or the walking wounded with cut fingers overflowing the treatment room? Are you going to stand gaping at me with your clothes on all day? Did you ever have rheumatism as a child or young adult? Any heart trouble? Ever feel sick or uncomfortable playing on swings or merry-go-rounds? Ever feel car-sick? Any abdominal surgery or hernias? Any TB in your family? Insanity, dizzy spells, headaches, syphilis, diabetes? Cough. Get dressed.

"Doctor Marshall will check your vision. A formality, that, unless you've gone blind since your pre-employment medical. Don't worry, Mr. Carson, you're fit. Tell your CFI I said so. *Next* . . . !"

During the eye test it was again impossible to do or say anything, but when they had returned to Marshall's office to record the results he said quickly, "I have a problem, Doctor. Or rather, my friend has a problem. I'm not going to put forward a hypothetical case which will turn out to be my own. Honest. I'd better start all over again. You have several years' psychiatric experience, isn't that so, Doctor?"

Marshall nodded. She looked through the window into the treatment room and said, "Mr. Carson, this will be a very short conversation or a long one with lots of breaks in it. What exactly *is* your problem, or your friend's problem?"

"I'm not sure," said Carson. He took a deep breath, then went on, "I've already spoken to you about him. John Pebbles, remember? I wanted to stop people playing tricks on him and getting him into trouble. Now he has been promoted and certain people are still using him to do their dirty work. By this I don't mean literally dirty, just work which involves the misdirection of expensive material by a few highly placed individuals within the company. I would not like to see an innocent man—and Pebbles, you'll agree, is about as innocent as they come—get into trouble . . ."

As he was speaking he felt oddly pleased that he was not telling lies to this girl. He was not telling the whole truth, either—but then Carson himself did not know the whole truth and the project *could* be described as the misdirection of material by highly placed Hart-Ewing personnel.

". . . All this is highly confidential," he ended seriously. "I would not tell you about it if I did not have to explain my interest in Pebbles."

She looked suddenly interested. "I don't see what else I can tell you that I haven't already told you. I'm not being difficult, Mr. Carson, I just don't know any more."

"But *I* know a lot more about him now, and I would like a professional opinion on what it all means . . ."

He went on quickly to describe John Pebbles as he had first appeared, standing open-mouthed and rain-soaked as he watched the club aircraft; as he had appeared at his pre-employment check, as he had been as a lavatory attendant and floor sweeper, and as he was now as a flying instructor and student of no mean ability. For a man registered as disabled through being metally retarded he had come a very long way very quickly. Carson wanted to know if this intellectual spurt was usual or even possible and, if it had been accomplished through sheer determination, it there was a danger of a sudden lapse or breakdown which would lose him everything he had gained. He would also like to know the incidence of mentally retarded cases who suddenly shot ahead like this?

When Carson finished she was silent for a long time, then she said doubtfully, "The answer to most of your questions, Mr. Carson, is: I don't know. But it seems to me that if he was retarded in the generally accepted sense, that is if his mentation at the age of thirty was still that of a child of six, then he could not possibly shoot ahead in the manner you describe. If he was simply a slow starter—a *very* slow starter—he should find it much more difficult to catch up.

"Unless," she added suddenly, "he is simply an amnesia victim."

Carson thought about that for a while, then said, "Did you ever work in the MacNaughton Clinic?"

"Yes," she said. "For three years before . . . Well, it's a long story."

Carson nodded. Her face was expressive as well as beautiful and he doubted if she could be bothered to hide her feelings at any time. It was obvious, therefore, that he had just touched a very sensitive spot. He wished suddenly that she did not look so much like a young and long-suffering nun . . .

Smiling, he said, "One of these fine week ends, Doctor,

I would dearly like to take you for a drive—if you don't have other arrangements, that is, or an even bigger and healthier boy friend. We could lunch at the club, watch everybody there envying me for a couple of hours and on the way back we might call at the Clinic to ask about—"

"One of these fine week ends," she broke in furiously "someone will forget that I'm a dedicated bloody angel of mercy and realize that—"

"But your dedication is all I can appeal to, Doctor," said Carson hastily, "until I know you better."

Chapter 11

He went to the club alone as usual that week end. Dr. Marshall had other arrangements made, but she said the following week end would be free. On arrival he discovered that Pebbles had not yet returned from his course and that Bob Maxwell would be flying with him.

Carson tried hard not to be unnerved by the presence of Maxwell in the cockpit—the chief flying instructor often flew with other instructors' pupils to check on the trainee-pilot's progress. Carson had simply been lucky up until now to have escaped what was generally considered to be a grueling practical examination of the pupil's flying ability, if any.

But Maxwell did not appear to be terribly interested in Carson's attempts to impress him with his expertise. Carson took a deep breath and decided to do everything by the book—always assuming, of course, that he could remember the contents . . .

When he closed the cockpit canopy and strapped in, he made a point of carefully checking Maxwell's straps as well—theoretically Carson was in charge and the responsibility for passenger safety was his. Unhurriedly, but trying not to show any sign of hesitation, he went through the first series of checks.

Brakes, on; fuel cock, on; standby fuel pump, on; generator switches, on; magnetos, both on; carburetor, heat; mixture, rich; throttle, primed once and set. He had a very careful—and ostentatious—look around to check that the area was clear, then pulled the starter and went into the pre-taxi checks.

Set throttle to give one thousand revs per minute and check that the friction nut was not too loose or tight. Altimeter set to zero feet. Directional gyro caged to avoid damage during taxi. Radio on at a comfortable volume. Carburetor, heat; mixture, rich. He increased the revs to fifteen hundred and switched to each magneto in turn, observing no serious drop in revs, then switched to both. He switched off the standby fuel pump and observed no effect on the fuel pressure gauge. Everything was fine. He set the trim, checked for free movement of flaps, ailerons and elevators, had another look around and unclipped the mike.

"Tango Zulu. Taxi," he said.

"Tango Zulu, you are clear to taxi to the holding point on runway Zero Four," said the tower in its most formal voice. They were trying to impress the CFI, too.

"Tango Zulu," acknowledged Carson. He had another ostentatious look around, released the brakes and opened the throttle.

At the holding point he angled the aircraft for a clear view of the runway and approaches, then locked the brakes. Hotel Sierra, the Cessna piloted by Jeff Donnelly, was beginning to turn on to finals. Carson began his pre-takeoff checks.

Set trim. Set throttle to fast tickover and check friction nut tightness again. Mixture rich and carb cold for maximum power. Standby fuel pump on in case the mechanical pump failed during takeoff and the engine went out. Fuel cock fully on and meter showing sufficient fuel for the flight. He set one-quarter flaps, the recommended setting for takeoff, rechecked the harness of Maxwell and himself and made sure the canopy was secure.

Carson relaxed then for a moment while Jeff Donnelly touched down smoothly and rolled to the end of the runway, then he radioed for and received permission to take off. He had another look around, released the brakes, moved smartly on to the center line of the runway and opened the throttle.

They went charging down the center of the runway with Carson working hard to keep them there. The ASI needle crept up towards sixty-five knots and he eased back on the control column. The wheels stopped rumbling and, relieved of ground drag, the aircraft picked up speed. They climbed away steadily with the airspeed indicator needle nailed firmly onto the seventy knots mark and the stall warning shamed into silence.

At three hundred feet he raised the flaps smoothly so as to avoid a sudden loss of altitude and switched off the standby fuel pump. The fuel gauge said that the mechanical pump was working perfectly. He continued the climb to six hundred feet, checked that the area was clear of other aircraft and made a climbing turn through ninety degrees to port. The angle subtended by the horizon and the lateral axis of the aircraft was no more than a degree plus or minus that required for a Rate One turn. He continued climbing and, anticipating slightly, eased the stick forward so that he leveled off at exactly one thousand feet.

He switched the carburetor to heat to prevent icing, closed the throttle until the ASI showed the recommended cruising speed of eighty knots. He scanned the area again, made another ninety-degree turn to port and flew downwind parallel to the runway. He unclipped the mike.

"Tango Zulu downwind," he said.

"Tango Zulu, you are clear to finals."

"Tango Zulu."

"Are you happy with this airplane, Mr. Carson?" said Maxwell suddenly.

Carson examined the question for implications. Perhaps he did not *look* happy with it. Maybe he was not flying it properly, in the CFI's opinion, and Maxwell was letting him know about it as tactfully as possible. Or perhaps he just wanted to know.

"I'm getting used to it," said Carson, "and I don't think I should change now. Do you?"

Maxwell ignored the question and asked another. "Are you happy with your instructor?"

"Yes," said Carson.

"You sound a trifle hesitant. Is he rough on you? Exacting? Insists on you doing all the work? Demands an unreasonably high standard of flying?"

"In order," said Carson, smiling, "the answers are yes, yes, yes and yes. I like him personally, what little I know of him, and as a pilot he is very, well, neat, about everything he does . . ."

"It rubs off," said Maxwell drily.

The end of the runway was just passing behind the port wing trailing edge. Carson looked around, then turned ninety degrees on to the base leg. He reduced power and put the nose down, judging his descent so that he would be about seven hundred feet up when he turned on to his final approach. He set one-half flap for landing and switched on the standby fuel pump in case he needed full power quickly. The patchwork of fields, roads, farmhouses and clumps of trees were slipping past faster now as he lost height. But his attention was on the runway stretching away to the left, paralleling his port wing.

He began a gradual turn to port while with the other hand he unclipped the mike and said, "Tango Zulu. Turning finals."

"Tango Zulu, you are clear to land on runway Zero Four."

"Tango Zulu."

He was turning a shade wide and he knew that Maxwell would not be impressed by an approach in the shape of a series of S-turns. He increased the bank until he was almost lined up with the center of the runway then smoothly took it off. The runway stretched ahead like a narrow, isoceles triangle—he was properly lined up! He began to drift very slightly to port and gave the starboard rudder just a hair of pressure. There was the beginning of a starboard drift so he gave the port rudder pedal half a hair. The ASI read seventy-five knots, his attitude was right so far, the engine was just ticking over and the main road was slipping under his nose. The runway was beginning to slide off to the side again . . .

"You are a shade tense, Mr. Carson," said Maxwell.

"The runway won't hold still," said Carson, edging it back to where it belonged. The isoceles triangle was becoming more equilateral. He had picked his spot to round out—a point about thirty yards beyond the white-painted numerals—and he watched it carefully. If it showed a tendency to move towards him and under the nose it meant he was overshooting. If it appeared to move away he was doing the opposite. It seemed to be creeping away from him very slightly, so he opened the throttle a little for a few seconds to reduce the angle of descent, then returned it to the tickover setting.

Applying power had caused the nose to go up as well as causing a slight yaw and port wing drop. He corrected all three. An updraft dropped the other wing. He corrected that. His round-out spot was staying put, so was the runway. The boundary hedge whipped past below him and the big 0 and 4 were rushing up . . .

He gave a strained laugh and sang tunelessly, "Oh Four the wings of a dove . . ."

"Oh God," said Maxwell, covering his face.

But the instructor's feet were still hovering over the rudder pedals and the hands covering his face had their fingers open so that he could still see, and the control column was within easy reach in an emergency.

This was the point where Carson bumped if he was going to bump. He either rounded out too high and dropped on to the runway to the accompaniment of jeering noises from the stall warning horn, or he came in too low and fast so that he touched down hard and bounced. The idea was to get as close to the ground as possible then fly straight and level above it. Theoretically, Pebbles was always telling him, there was no difference between flying accurately at one thousand feet and one foot.

Carson thought his altitude was one foot but he did not *know*. He was centered on the runway with wings level and airspeed dropping away. He brought the nose up gently to hold off for as long as possible. It seemed as though he had been flying a few inches above the runway for hours. He eased the nose up a little more—the ASI showed a figure close to stalling speed—and felt the aircraft begin to sink . . .

There was no bump, just a beautiful, continuous rumble of wheels on tarmac.

"An acceptable landing," said Maxwell. "Let me see you do it again."

Carson put the carburetor on cold, opened the throttle while they were still rolling at speed along the runway and did it all again. When they were down he said, "Round again?"

Maxwell shook his head. "Stop at the end of the runway and let me off, then try it yourself. Just one circuit, mind. And don't worry, Mr. Carson, you'll be all right." He laughed suddenly. "I'll stand on the end of the runway to hold it steady while you come in . . ."

If anything Carson was even more careful while he was doing it by himself. He knew that the CFI was at the end of the runway observing every move. The tower, which would have seen Maxwell leave the airplane and would know that Carson was making his first solo, would be watching him through binoculars. They would also have passed the news to everyone in the clubhouse. The bar would be getting ready for the round of drinks Carson would buy to mark this great occasion and for the party which usually developed afterwards.

There was only one moment on the downwind leg when Carson became frightened, when he wondered what he was doing up here all alone. Then he saw the grounds and tiny, bright buildings of the MacNaughton Clinic and the fields stretching between it and the airfield, and he became angry rather than frightened.

All this had come about as a direct result of his efforts to investigate the project through its supposedly weak mental link. But now flying had become very important to Carson and he felt terribly wrong, somehow, about mixing security business with pleasure. Pebbles had taught him to fly. The shy, stammering, intensely reserved Pebbles who was now beginning to look as if he might be something much more than a weak link.

Top pilots were made and not born. They were made from the very best physical and mental material, and Pebbles was certainly in the top class. They were *not* made from the kind of material which Pebbles purported to be and they were not patients at establishments like the Mac-Naughton Clinic. Pebbles was to have been his means of learning the details and ultimate purpose of the project so that he could protect it.

Now he was beginning to wonder if Pebbles was the man he should be protecting it from . . .

Angrily he wondered why his suspicions had chosen this particular moment to crystallize, taking the edge off the excitement and joy of his first solo. In a few seconds he would have to clear his mind for the approach and landing. Pleasure and business did not mix. But it came as a surprise to him that his strongest feeling towards Pebbles, even stronger than the anger, was one of gratitude.

Even if Pebbles was a spy with all that that implied, Carson felt sure that the feeling would stay with him all his life.

Later in the clubhouse he was surprised to see Wayne Tillotson among the crowd of insulting, back-slapping, arm-punching well-wishers—not so much surprised at his presence than at his appearance.

Tillotson's voice was slurred as he said, "Hurry up and buy me that drink, Joe, so I can buy you one. I'm having a party, too, you know—no special reason. And congratulations. It's a pity John couldn't be here. He told me that you were ready to go solo . . ."

"He didn't tell me," said Carson drily.

Carson had never seen Tillotson drunk before or even heard of him getting drunk. But it was a condition which made for useful slips of the tongue—always provided, of course, that he could steer the conversation onto the right topic. He went on thoughtfully, "I wish he would talk more —about himself, I mean. I like him a lot, but I wish he would open up sometimes. I think he has problems..."

Back to business ...

Chapter 12

The file in the dirty envelope at the bottom of his junk drawer grew thicker, but slowly. Carson's frustration was fast reaching the pitch where he was about to hang the consequences and *make* something happen. One reason for not doing so was that his opposite number might react violently when he discovered that an outsider knew about the project—he kept remembering Herbie Patterson, and wondering. The other reason was that Carson, in his own cynical fashion, regarded himself as a patriot and he was still not sure whether the project would be best served by his silence or by his ignorant and perhaps misguided efforts at protecting it.

From Pebbles?

He still could not make up his mind about that.

As a result he continued his wanderings all over the Hart-Ewing complex when by rights he should have been in his office, and working late nights to clear the paperwork and to visit empty offices and departments which might contain useful information. But the odd pieces he was able to pick up merely filled in the edges of the puzzle; they gave no idea of the shape and subject of the picture.

He called several times on Pebbles only to find him too busy to do more than exchange the time of day. But on one occasion he managed a hurried invitation to the flat for the beer that was still due him. Pebbles wavered for a moment then accepted, although he did not set a time. It was progress, however, but slow.

At the pilots' offices he was told that Wayne Tillotson had gone off somewhere on a special course and would not be back for at least a week.

It had been a peculiar party for the clubhouse where as a rule nobody drank to excess. Tillotson had hit the bottle like a backsliding alcoholic. He had hit a great many bottles with a wide variety of contents. He had arrived in a taxi instead of his sports car and another cab had taken the remains home.

There had been a quality almost of desperation about the way he had filled himself with everything which would pour while he talked to everyone in sight. To Carson he had talked a lot about Pebbles as he had been in the early days, and he discovered that Tillotson was the only person who had been to Pebbles' place or had the other visit him. Wayne was his only real friend, it seemed, but just before the test pilot passed out he had about-faced and insisted to Carson that he was *not* the poor dope's best friend because as a result of his kindness Pebbles was going to get himself killed or worse . . .

Offhand, Carson knew of only one fate worse than death, but he was fairly certain that Tillotson had not been thinking of that.

Which left Dr. Marshall.

He drove over to collect her shortly after lunch on the following Sunday. It was a scorching hot day without cloud or wind except for that generated by the speed of his freshly washed and polished car. His sports jacket was quietly resplendent, the creases in his slacks were suitably knife-edged and he had shaved to within an inch of his life and at a point just below his ear even closer than that.

The Marshall house was fairly small with a large back garden, both of which were being noisily overrun by young children—only two children, Carson was surprised to discover when he counted heads. The doctor's brother met him at the door and asked him in for a beer while he was waiting. That was only the first of many questions, questions which could have been irritating if not downright embarrassing if Gordon Marshall had not been equally free with his answers.

Gordon, he discovered, was the man of the house and took his duties seriously. His father had died recently after a long illness. His sister Jean had been looking after their father since their mother, who had been crippled as the result of a car accident for over six years, had died early last year. They had not needed the services of a full-time doctor, of course, but there had still been an awful lot for Jean to do when she came off duty at the clinic. That was why she had moved to Hart-Ewing with its shorter and more regular hours. She did not have so much to do at home these days, but it was a great consolation to have a doctor in the house, especially when Gordon's wife had been expecting...

Gordon did not say that his big sister was in danger of becoming an old maid. Neither did he say that the house was too small for a growing family, that his sister and wife, who was pregnant again, had arguments in which he was forced to take sides or that it was impossible for his wife and himself to periodically clear the air with a good old-fashioned row without Jean overhearing it. He did not say any of these things and, Carson was sure, he was not even aware of not saying them. It was just that Carson had become expert at listening between the lines.

It was only when Gordon began asking detailed personal questions about his medical history and parents that Carson felt impelled to react.

"Take it easy, Gordon," he said, laughing. "I realize that you feel it necessary to check on your sister's men friends—as a stand-in for your father, perhaps—and I also realize that in a medically oriented household questions regarding matters of health might tend to be, well, explicit. But aren't you jumping the gun a little, considering this is the first time I have taken her out?"

Gordon laughed, too, but uncomfortably. He said, "I didn't think I was being so obvious, Joe. I'm sorry. And it isn't me you have to worry about, it's her. The third degree was simply to find out if we would see you around again. Once has usually been enough for the others to decide that they didn't measure up.

"I hope I'm not scaring you off, Joe," he went on. "She isn't nasty or very bad-tempered or anything like that. It's just that she has this peculiar kink about not getting emotionally involved with a man who may turn out to be just another patient . . ."

He broke off and looked past Carson towards the living room door, his eyebrows going up. He murmured, "She doesn't usually go to all this trouble. Maybe we will see you next Sunday, after all . . ."

Carson turned as he rose to his feet. He had been expecting Jean Marshall to look different but not necessarily better. Any girl in a doctor or nurse's whites had things going for her which transcended the purely physical attractions. The crisp whites symbolized the many admirable qualities demanded by her profession and gave her an attraction which was both real and invisible. But very often when she changed into street clothes, even though she was exactly the same person possessing the same qualities, she became just another plain girl in the street.

Jean Marshall was dressed plainly but she did not look plain. The sandals were little more than holes held together with thin straps revealing feet that Carson would probably have drooled over had he been a foot fetishist. Her dark blue slacks were not overly tight and her white sweater was not sloppy enough to hide anything either. Her sleeves were pulled up to just below the elbows and she carried a swimsuit wrapped in a towel in one hand. Carson would not have minded betting that she had spent more time on her face and hair making it look un-made-up than he had on his car trying to make it look new, and to much better effect.

"Oh, brother," he said softly.

"In-law," said Gordon, laughing. "If you're not careful, Joe, it will be in-law . . ."

When they were on the outskirts of town and with a few miles to go before the turn-off for the coast, unselfishness reared its beautiful head. Carson had been determined to take her for a drive along the coast, then to the club for a meal and finally to the Clinic—just to prove to her that he was taking her out for reasons other than a means of gaining access to the hospital. She, on the other hand, insisted that they go to the Clinic first because he was concerned about Pebbles and would probably be able to enjoy himself more if that particular worry was removed. Carson replied that he would not mind missing the hospital altogether and putting off their visit until next week —besides being the right thing to say, it was almost true. But she became quite insistent and to avoid an argument he had to be selfish and go to the Clinic first.

It was like offering cigarettes in a crowd—the one who was slowest on the draw won.

The MacNaughton Clinic had a large gate but very low walls. Generally speaking, the patients had neither the ability nor the inclination to leave and the people of the outside world had no wish to go anywhere near the place. The gates were open, the driveway clear and the grounds empty. All the activity was centered around three large buses drawn up in front of the main building.

"Take the next on the right, Joe," Jean said, "then second left. We'll go in by the back door."

The "back door" opened into a network of bright, cool corridors smelling of the usual hospital combination of antiseptic and floor polish. There was nobody in sight. They were about to move to the next floor when they heard footsteps coming down the stairs three at a time.

"Doctor Morris!" called Jean.

A small, wiry figure in a discordant sportshirt who was on the way down the stairs stumbled, took four and two instead of two threes, but still managed to land upright at the bottom.

"Marshall!" it said in a surprisingly resonant bass. "Jean, it's nice to see you again. What are you doing here anyway? And who is your large friend?"

"Joe Carson," said Carson, shaking hands, "from Hart-Ewing. I wanted some information about a one-time patient of yours. John Pebbles."

"Is he in trouble?"

Carson shook his head. "He is doing very well. But he had problems which, for some reason, he won't let me help him with. I wanted to talk to someone who knew him when he first arrived here. That was before Jean's time here but she offered to—"

"Of course, Doctor," said Morris. "But the one you should talk to is Nurse Sampson. Unfortunately, she left on the first coach. Unless you fancy a trip with us to the beach, and in the circumstances we would understand if you refused, you'll have to come back later this evening."

"We were planning on going for a swim," said Carson, "so we might as well mix business with pleasure. But I should explain that I'm not . . ."

He did not get a chance to explain that he was not a doctor because Morris was already trotting towards the entrance, calling back that they should follow the last bus which would be leaving in ten minutes.

On the way to the coast they had the choice of being boiled alive in their own body juices or opening the car windows and eating the bus dust, so they alternated by doing both. By the time they arrived at the narrow and secluded stretch of beach Carson was looking forward to a swim. But there was work to do first, Jean told him, and suggested that he change in the car while she found out how best they could help.

It was rather like setting up butchers' stalls in a marketplace.

First they unrolled the gaily colored wind breakers and pushed their supporting poles into the soft sand, then they unfolded and positioned the deck chairs. The . . . goods . . . were carried out of the buses then, carefully but awkwardly, and put on display in the deck chairs like so many lumpy pink sacks with furiously talking heads on top. They seemed to talk all the time but that was probably because they were capable of doing nothing else.

During the first few minutes Carson thought he was going to be sick. The close, almost intimate contact with the bodies—they had been dressed for the beach before being loaded into the buses—was bad. The horrible *lightness* of these people—arms and legs, it seemed, accounted for about half of a person's body weight—was even worse. But worst of all was the way they talked and joked with him, especially the girls. But gradually the feeling passed as he worked, until eventually he was able to arrange the pink bundles on their deck chairs as though he had been doing it all his life, and even rub suntan lotion on some of them.

He wondered if he was an adaptable, sympathetic type or just insensitive.

During a pause for breath before starting to unload the last bus, Carson nodded towards the two muscular male nurses who were sitting back to back on the bus roof, looking through binoculars. He said, "We could use some help."

Jean laughed. "Do I detect a note of criticism, Joe? But seriously, those two are our deterrent. We don't often need them because most people know this section of the beach is reserved for us and they wouldn't come within miles of us in any case. But there are others who would and sometimes they even carry cameras. When that kind turns up the boys go out to meet them and dissuade them from coming too close. Sometimes their telephoto lenses are heaved into the sea or they get sand in the works of their expensive cameras, and there are times when the action is even more direct. The boys feel very strongly about that particular type of Peeping Tom . . . "

Carson said, "My criticism is disarmed by your deterrents. Now let's unload this bunch so's we can cool off in the sea . . . "

But by the time they had unloaded the last bus the people on the deck chairs wanted to cool off in the sea as

87

well. This was the best part of the outing. Instead of the Clinic's tiny swimming pool with its clutter of special floats and harnesses, here were real breakers, acres of hot sand and thousands of smooth, brightly-colored pebbles. They did not have arms or legs, so they had to be carried into the sea, and because they could not swim without them they had to be dunked and splashed and towed around the shallows. All except one, that was, who had fingerless hands growing out of her shoulders and who could swim like a tail-less fish.

She was enjoying herself so much, they were all enjoying themselves so much, that Carson wanted to curse horribly just to relieve his feelings. Normally he did not consider himself a particularly fortunate man, but right now he felt so lucky that it was almost a physical pain.

The pain remained with him for the succeeding two hours, during which patients were dunked, floated, towed, chased, returned to their chairs and dried. It made it impossible for him to think of anything else, so much so that it was Dr. Morris who brought his mind back to the reason for his being here.

"I expect you two had your own plans for the rest of the day," he said to Carson while his eyes wandered admiringly along Jean who lay between them on the sand. "We're grateful for your help but we don't want to work you to death. You can leave any time you feel like it, Doctors. But before you go, you wanted to ask about John Pebbles, Joe . . . "

Carson pushed himself onto one elbow and looked down at Jean. She was smiling faintly, eyes closed and obviously waiting to see how, or if, he would extricate himself. He said awkwardly, "I'm not a doctor, Doctor. Not even a psychologist . . . "

Morris stared at him for an uncomfortable three seconds, then said, "You could have fooled me, Joe. But you wanted to know about Pebbles." He broke off for a moment to whistle, wave and beckon to someone further along the beach. Carson turned to see a small girl in a yellow swimsuit wave back, then move towards them. She was beautiful by any man's standards, with skin like smooth dark chocolate. Morris went on, "He liked her more than any of us—thought she was different, for obvious reasons. She liked him, too, and took special care of him. It was she who found him, after all."

"Nurse Sampson," he said as she stopped above them, "will be able to tell you everything you want to know about John Pebbles . . ."

Chapter 13

It had happened more than four years before in the early spring. Because the weather was too cold for swimming the patients had been wrapped warmly in rugs and since they needed little attention, Nurse Sampson had gone for a walk along the beach to the little bay about half a mile along the coast. It was an attractive spot, but unsuitable for swimming because of the sharp rocks lying beneath the surface, the seaweed which clung to them, and the carpet of stones covering the spaces between.

She had found him curled up birthday-naked on the sheltered side of a rocky outcropping. At the time she had thought only of the patient, assuming he was exhausted after swimming ashore from a sunken motorboat or yacht. When she remembered about the clothing which might have helped identify him, the tide must have washed it away. All she noticed at the time was a large, torn sheet of bright orange plastic material. She had thought that it was part of a rubber dinghy at first, but the material was different. There had been no lettering or serial numbers on the plastic so far as she had been able to see.

She had lifted him clear of the water, which had begun to wash over his legs, wrapped her coat around him and run for help.

The thing she remembered most clearly about the inci-

dent was the difficulty they had getting his right hand un-
clenched. It had contained five small, brightly colored
pebbles from the beach and he had cried like a baby when
they tried to take them away. He still had them with him
when he left the Clinic eight months later.

On that first day his physical condition was all that concerned them. As well as suffering from exposure, incip-
ient pneumonia and widespread lacerations and abrasions to his hands, arms, elbows, knees and shins caused by
crawling—he did not know how to walk—over rocks, he
had cried a lot. It had been the completely unashamed
crying of someone who did not know or had never learned
about stiff upper lips.

Gradually as the abrasions healed and his surroundings
became more comfortable and familiar, he cried only when
he was hungry or faced with a similiar form of personal
emergency. He had no more control over his motions
than a baby, he did not understand a single word spoken
to him, and he replied to everything that was said with
gurgles or other nonsense sounds. He had to be taught to
do *everything*.

His physical coordination was very good, however. He
learned how to stand and sit and walk about very quickly.
In two months he could go to the toilet unaided, in three
he could eat without making too great a mess of the table-
top and when he had been at the clinic six months, Nurse
Sampson arranged a party for him at which he was able
to make a very short speech and read five pages from a
book intended for five-year-olds. During the whole of his
stay he had displayed the intense, innocent curiosity of a
small boy. He had no illnesses of any kind and the minor
injuries he had sustained were usually caused by trying to
climb trees, drainpipes and furniture.

He began to wander, disappearing from the hospital for
hours at a time, but he always came back. He was always
muddy and excited and quite incoherent about whatever
it was he had been doing. His independent trips outside
seemed to help his condition, he seemed to be avoiding
trouble or injury, and so they were encouraged.

Then one afternoon he had returned with a friend in tow—literally pulling him up the Clinic steps like a newly-discovered uncle he wanted to show off. The friend's name had been Tillotson and from him they had discovered among other things what John Pebbles had been doing during his twice-daily disappearances. Tillotson was rather embarrassed at the raw hero-worship Pebbles displayed towards him, but this had not stopped him putting forward a strong case for the other's discharge from the hospital. Tillotson had insisted that Pebbles was much brighter than he seemed, that he could almost certainly wangle him a job in surroundings which he would find pleasant and that it was wrong, anyway, to institutionalize people unnecessarily.

Tillotson could have saved his breath and his eloquence because he was preaching to the converted . . .

" . . . We kept him for another four weeks," Nurse Sampson went on, "giving him an intensive survival course—you know, how to get on and off buses and trains, how to judge the speed and direction of traffic, reading traffic lights, that sort of thing. Finally we turned him loose on the world."

Her teeth were dazzling as she smiled, but from her tone it was obvious that Nurse Sampson had been very sorry to see Pebbles go.

Morris joined in then. Defensively, he said, "We aren't being callous about this, Joe. It's just that the Clinic gets the really bad cases, the ones who have no chance of making it in the outside world even with complicated harnesses or gadgetry. We're very glad about Pebbles, but too busy with the failures to take a close interest. In any case, Dr. Kennedy and Mr. Savage at Hart-Ewing promised to let us know if John ran into any trouble. They haven't and now you tell me he hasn't . . . "

"He has done very well," said Carson. He was convinced, without knowing why, that if he told Morris and the nurse just how well that was he would not be believed. He went on carefully, "He has been doing very well at night school and he doesn't sweep floors anymore. But the thing which intrigues me is where he came from originally. Had you any luck tracing his parents or relatives?"

"The chances are that they didn't want to be traced," said Morris. "That does not necessarily mean that they were heartless or callous, either. I can imagine circumstances where taking care of him properly could be too much for ordinary people. Physically he was very well cared for and there was no evidence of cruelty. But whoever was responsible for bringing him up from a baby could have been about to succumb to illness or old age, or have been about to marry, or just have decided that he might do better under the care of professionals. Which he did.

"At first we thought he might be a simple amnesiac," the doctor went on, "but there were no signs of head injuries and it is unusual for amnesia to be so complete without massive injury to the brain. I don't think it was intended for him to take off his clothes or cut himself on the rocks—he must have crawled away from the place he had been left at, where we would probably have found him much sooner. As I said, he had been very well fed and cared for and we didn't want to raise a stink with the police over a case of unintentional cruelty, so we looked after him and kept quiet about it."

"If he wasn't suffering from amnesia," said Carson, "what was his trouble, Doctor?"

"Amnesia is not completely ruled out, Joe. But total loss of memory is uncommon. It is usually caused by severe brain injury or a very severe traumatic shock, but even then the loss is not total because the patient can still talk and eat and dress himself, even though he may not know who he is or recognize any of his friends for a time. Unless there is physical damage to the brain, surrounding the patient with friends and familiar objects will usually bring his memory back, and there is medication available these days which aids the remembering process. We tried both forms of treatment with Pebbles, even though we could not know what he would have considered familiar surroundings or people."

93

The doctor wriggled a little deeper into the warm sand, then went on, "In some areas he responded quickly— learning to walk, dress, open doors and so on. He *could* have picked these up quickly because he already had known how and the memories were coming back—familiar surroundings and activities can bring an amnesiac's memory rushing back, sometimes. But he had forgotten how to *speak*. No amount of talking at him would bring that memory back, and that is the one ability which is very rarely forgotten even by so-called 'total' amnesia cases. We had to teach him as if he was learning a new language—at no stage did he show signs of prior knowledge or familiarity with it. That is why I'm not happy about the amnesia theory.

"There were no indications of physical damage," Morris concluded, "and a purely mental shock which would give those symptoms is something which does not bear thinking about."

"I suppose," said Carson a few minutes later, "that he could not have been pretending to have forgotten everything . . . "

Immediately he knew that he had said the wrong thing —it was suddenly very chilly on the hot sand. Even Jean was looking coldly at him. He went on quickly. "Obviously the answer is no. But quite apart from the fact that he was dumped on you like a thirty-year-old foundling, he was and is an unusual case. My mouth may be full of foot again, but there is one more question I'd like to ask and it's this: Bearing in mind the facts that he showed no signs of physical injury or neglect, that his symptoms were not those of a normal amnesiac and that, with loving care, good tuition and proper medical attention you were able to bring him along to the point where he is now able to live a fairly normal life, is it possible that he was not born the way you found him? Could some of the drugs you used to support his therapy have been misused to leave him in that condition? Could his memory have been obliterated deliberately, or perhaps by accident as the result of an experiment which went wrong? Could he have been a volunteer who—"

"For God's *sake* . . . !"

Morris sat bolt upright, showering them with sand. He went on, "So instead of being left by relatives who could no longer cope with looking after him for thirty-odd years, you are suggesting that he is a waste product of a too-efficient brain-washing experiment left with us for possible salvage? You've got a too-vivid imagination, Joe, and I wish to blazes you wouldn't put such uncomfortable thoughts into people's minds . . . !"

Jean and he dressed and left shortly afterwards. In the car neither of them spoke as Carson drove towards the airfield. Suddenly he pulled into a side road, let the car coast until they were in the shade of some overhanging trees, then he braked and switched the motor off, still without speaking.

"You looked bothered and your hands are shaking," she said when the silence had grown so long and deep that the insects were beginning to sound noisy. "Is it passion or delayed shock?"

Carson did not answer.

"I was a bit rough on you, letting you go with them to the beach," she went on apologetically. "But there are far too many people who just don't want to know about the Clinic's patients—if they don't know, then nobody can accuse them of not caring, I suppose. But it was bound to be a shock for you, seeing and handling really bad thalidomide and dystrophy cases. I thought you were taking it very well and I'm sorry if . . . Joe, are you going to sit and sulk all day . . . !"

Carson said, "What did you say?"

He had heard every word, but he had been feeling so angry and betrayed and disgusted that the meaning of the words had seemed to slide past him. He had also been coming to a decision which was completely at variance with everything he had ever been taught as a security man. But he badly needed help of a very specialized kind, and instinctively he knew that time was running too short for him to get it by the roundabout methods he had been using over the past weeks. Without telling Jean Marshall everything—he could withhold the names and the nature of the project—he might still be able to get the help he needed in exposing John Pebbles for what he was.

Even though the man might not know what he was himself . . .

He said suddenly, "I'm not sulking, Jean. I was going to spend the rest of the day at the flying club, where I would have let you watch me doing good take-offs and very bad landings after which I would have plied you with booze during dinner and taken you home—yours or mine, depending on the psychological effects of the alcohol in your bloodstream . . . "

Just to make sure that she knew he was joking, Carson laughed. It sounded forced even to him, and his hands were shaking again. He dropped them onto his lap, surrepetitiously rubbing the sweat off his palms, and went on. "But Pebbles will be at the club. After what I found out at the beach I don't want to see him for a while. I—I've something to tell you about Pebbles, and the reason I've wanted to see him as much as possible." Instinctively he reached towards her and took her hand. It felt warm and smooth and firm, but completely unresponsive. "You're a doctor, Jean, so I'm sure you will treat this as privileged information. You see, this thing has been troubling me for some time and I need expert advice . . . "

He broke off because she was trying to pull her hand away. When he would not let go she said in a voice of quiet fury, "So you need a doctor, Joe? There are a lot of people like you around and I seem to run into all of them! Big, grown, healthy men who want round-the-clock medicare as well as a woman! Men so unsure of themselves that they want to hold a girl—if they want to hold a *girl* —by her professional ethics as well as love. I thought you might be different. You're fit and you haven't, until now, that is, started to complain about your mental problems. I thought you might be using your interest in John Pebbles

96

and my psychiatric training as an excuse to get to know me better . . . "

"I was, but I still need help with—"

" . . . But you might as well know right now," she went on furiously, "that I am not going to be anyone's private doctor! My patients get care and attention and first-class treatment—I'm good at my job—but they get nothing else. Men who take me out because they think medical people are morally lax are bad enough. The ones who think that the only subject of conversation of interest to me is physical ailments, *their* physical ailments, naturally, are worse. But the ones who know my background and want some cut-price psychiatry, the ones whose troubles are mental rather than physical and insist on bearing the innermost, murky recesses of their souls—pretty normal, average souls if they only knew it—these I find particularly . . . disappointing.

"You may think me some kind of nut myself for feeling so strongly about this . . . "

Carson shook his head but did not speak. He had been arguing himself into telling her about the project and she had misunderstood to such a ridiculous extent that he did not know whether to laugh or yell at her to shut up. Instinctively he knew that both reactions would be wrong, and he cursed under his breath because he was being sidetracked again just as he thought he was getting somewhere. First the flying lessons and now Jean were diverting him from his original purpose.

" . . . had to look after two very sick relatives at night and strangers during the day," Jean was saying, quietly now and much more seriously. "My profession is a little like that of a policeman's—I'm on call at all times. Professionally I'm very sympathetic and helpful and a much nicer person generally, and possibly you will prefer the professional me for the short time you choose to be my patient. So if there is something really serious troubling you, Joe, some particularly shameful crime you think you are guilty of—"

"I'm not guilty of any shameful crime," Carson broke in

97

harshly, "unless you want to count high treason and counter counter-espionage! Let me get a word in edgewise, dammit! I thought, being the kind of person you are, that an appeal to your professional ethics would be better than waving the Official Secrets act to keep you from talking out of turn. You see, there is a very secret project at Hart-Ewing, so important and secret that even the chief security officer is not supposed to know about it. Recently I have become convinced that its security has been penetrated. I'm not sure how, exactly, and that is why I need your advice."

He hesitated, then went on carefully, "I'd prefer not to talk about it here and we can't go to the club. Besides, it's getting late and you must be hungry. I'm quite good with a can-opener, you know, and I wondered if we might go to my place to talk about it . . . ?"

"High treason beats etchings," she said after a long pause. Carson chose to treat it as an acquiescence and started the car.

But she was curious enough to insist on talking about it during the trip back and, because his concentration on the traffic weakened the guard on his tongue, by the time they reached the flat she knew almost as much as he did about the project.

Some security man he was turning out to be!

The subject was shelved while he showed her his books, his tape-recorders, hi-fi, records, assorted pieces of home carpentry and other junk. She said that she was impressed by the tidy heaps he kept his junk in.

In the kitchen he said madly unoriginal things about what a good wife he would make somebody, and the superficial, pseudo-domestic conversation continued until they had eaten and cleared away. Then Carson switched on the TV, but turned down the sound, saying that he just wanted to catch the news when it came on in a few minutes' time, and indicated the couch, saying that it was the most comfortable thing in the room because he had not made it himself.

She sat down on the edge and Carson sat beside her.

She looked at his arm lying along the back of the couch behind her and said, "What's this . . . ?"

He said, "If you look at it closely, which you are doing, you will see that it bends at the shoulder, elbow and wrist and that one end is fitted with five strong and highly flexible digits which are capable of a wide range of activities from stroking your hair to grabbing your slender, sunburned neck and choking off your piteous cries for help. Or if you prefer to treat it professionally, you may wish to take its pulse . . . "

She said something very unladylike about its pulse and lay back against his arm.

"I've got another just like it," said Carson, turning towards her and slipping his other hand around her waist. Before she could say anything, he bent forward and kissed her, long and thoroughly.

She tried to struggle free at first, but gradually she relaxed. He felt her wriggle into a more comfortable position, felt her free arm go around him and cool fingers on the back of his neck. By the time they broke for breath, Carson was well and truly sidetracked and what was more, he did not care. But when he pulled her close again she shook her head.

"Joe, you're bending my rib-cage. We . . . you wanted to talk about Pebbles . . . "

Carson said something very ungentlemanlike about Pebbles.

Seriously she went on, "Are you sure John Pebbles is a spy? I only saw him once but, well, I liked him. It's hard to believe that—"

"I've met him often," said Carson, still breathing hard, "and like him, too. But this is really important work Hart-Ewing is engaged in, and penetrating such a project calls for long and careful preparations and a spy with finesse. Perhaps the other side are finessing to such an extent that their spy does not even know that he is a spy. He might simply be a walking, strategically placed sponge absorbing information which means nothing to him until whatever conditioning was used on him to wipe his mind clean is reversed and they squeeze him dry.

"But the project's penetration might also require a spy with highly specialized knowledge and training . . ."

She was watching him intently, her face still only a few inches away, and Carson knew that if he was not careful he would get sidetracked again. He swallowed and went on, "Leaving Pebbles on the beach where the Clinic people would find him, maneuvering him into a boarding house run by a woman whose son had . . . Well, I'm afraid that I can't be sufficiently objective about this thing to admire them for it. Nobody would think of looking beyond the Clinic during the cursory security check we give lower-grade employees, and he started at a *very* low grade.

"But Dr. Morris said some very interesting things on the general subject of amnesia," he continued, "and I have a theory which needs your help to prove or disprove it. Morris said that an amnesia victim's memory is helped back by surrounding him with familiar objects, events and people. Now, Pebbles' progress was reasonably good so far as walking, opening doors, using a knife and fork and so on was concerned, but learning to talk and read took very much longer to learn. Another point—an important one, I think—was that he started making *real* progress only after he became interested in the club and landed the job with Hart-Ewing.

"Familiar surroundings, do you think?"

Without waiting for a reply he rushed on, "I didn't tell Dr. Morris about his meteoric rise foom floor-sweeper to qualified flying instructor because I doubt if he would have believed me. Pebbles is physically perfect, he has unusually fast reflexes and a sort of—of *authority* in the air which belongs only to top pilots. And now Tillotson, or someone else attached to the project who thinks he can use him, has wangled him an even more responsible job.

"I'm pretty sure that it is a space project and he, if my suspicions are correct, is a very specialized spy. It makes me wonder what exactly he was trained to do before his mind was wiped clean. Astronauts are *never* born and they are made with even greater difficulty than a top pilot. What will he do and say when his mind is switched on again? I want to know and to be able to take steps to protect the project. The only reason I've told you all about it and risked getting you as well as myself into serious trouble is that I'm convinced that we will find out in a very short time."

He took a deep breath, then concluded, "Flying and the aerospace industry are familiar ground to him. Would you agree that he is simply going over that ground again, doing revision? Reading and talking came much harder to him. Could that be because he was learning a foreign language?"

He had her undivided attention, but suddenly he lost it—she was staring past him at the TV. He swung around to see that the news had come on and that a still of Wayne Tillotson was smiling at him out of the screen. He reached forward and turned up the sound.

" . . . chief test pilot of Hart-Ewing, who is thought to have come down in the sea just before three-thirty this afternoon. The latest information to be released is that he radioed that he was having engine trouble but so far nothing further has been heard from him. The wreckage of the aircraft has not yet been sighted.

"Earlier this afternoon an unmanned Perseus series capsule burned up on re-entry when . . ."

Carson switched it off and sat back. They looked at each other without speaking. Jean's face reflected the minor-key shock and sorrow felt at the death of someone who is known and liked without being a close friend, while Carson was remembering that frantic party when he had begun to really know and like Tillotson. He was quite sure, without knowing why, that Wayne Tillotson had died in the returning Perseus capsule and not in an imaginary aircraft whose wreckage would never be found.

Partly to take his mind off the manner of the test pilot's death, he thought about the probable effects on the project.

Tillotson had been a key man. At very least the project personnel would be shaken, knocked off their stride, by his death. For the next few days their security might be less than tight and he might be able to take advantage of that . . .

The door-bell rang.

It was John Pebbles, looking shaken and very much off his stride. Someone—Dr. Morris or Nurse Sampson or maybe Wayne Tillotson—must have told him that big boys do not cry, but he was close to forgetting everything he had been told as the words came tumbling out.

He was stammering and trying to talk before Carson had finished opening the door—about Tillotson, about Carson's earlier invitation to the flat, about Carson's absence from the club today, about Tillotson's help over the years. Apart from the test pilot he did not know anyone well except Joe Carson—he had come here because he did not know what else to do. He babbled on about having nightmares and peculiar dreams and headaches. Mr. Tillotson had mentioned his seeing a psychiatrist but he was afraid of going back to the Clinic and not being allowed to fly or practice in the capsule . . .

He broke off as he saw Jean Marshall, looked appealingly at Carson, then began to back out, mumbling that he did not want to come in. Carson gripped his arm firmly and drew him inside.

"You're not intruding, John," he said, thinking that Nurse Sampson and Dr. Morris had been right—*nobody* could put on an act as good as this. His spy, who did not know that he was a spy, was really suffering and Carson felt himself torn between wanting to help console him and wanting to find out everything he could. He went on, "You've already met Dr. Marshall. There is no need to be afraid of her. Sit down and get it off your chest, and don't worry about going back to the Clinic or psychiatrists—a

102

friend is as good as a psychiatrist. Just tell us whatever it is that troubles you, as well as Wayne's death, of course. Jean won't mind. She tells me that she is always on duty."

"Yes," said Jean quietly, "just like a policeman . . ."

Chapter 14

He had been building up a reputation as a gossiping old woman, and now that he had changed his lunch break to coincide with Jean's and they began sitting together every day, his reputation was beginning to change and be envied. If some of the people who were currently watching them had known that during the past three evenings she had spent something like six hours in his flat, they would have been really envious, but without reason. Then, as now, she had been cool, pleasant and professional.

"I taped the conversation last night after you left," Carson said, "so you won't have to rely on hearsay evidence from a layman. He really does have a complicated dream life, and the way he described some of the sequences was even weirder than the dream themselves. If you could come over tonight and listen . . ."

"I'll come," she said, "but I think we're taking a risk being there together nearly every night he comes to see you. He's innocent but not stupid. One of these nights he will either decide that he is intruding and not come back, or he will realize that our guilty looks are due to our talking about him rather than because we may have been doing something to feel guilty about . . ."

Carson said, "Would you feel better if we did do something we should feel guilty about? I know I would."

"Be serious, Joe. What are we trying to do to John Pebbles? Get him shot, locked up? Right now he isn't guilty of anything and we both know it."

"The way you should look at it," said Carson, "is that if we're successful he won't be guilty because we will have prevented him from committing a crime.

"I'm going to work late tonight," he added, "so don't come until after nine o'clock. Tonight there is a project meeting and I intend doing a little eavesdropping . . ."

"You're taking a risk."

"Probably, but not a big one. Besides, I have to take some risks if we want to find out what exactly it is that we're investigating. You *do* believe that we are investigating something?"

"You are," said Jean coolly. "I am merely an advisor."

Carson practiced restraint for a few seconds, then said, "In a way this business is a little like coming in at the middle of a movie. By observing the actions and relationships of the characters it should be possible to deduce what has happened at the beginning of the film as it moves towards its climax. In a sense we are moving in two directions at once going simultaneously into the past and future. With Pebbles we have gone back very close to the beginning. If there is any order, any symmetry at all in the universe, we *must* be very close to the end . . ."

"Part of my advice," Jean went on as if he had not spoken, "is not to take too many risks."

But he took a risk later that afternoon when he rang Simpson in Publicity with a rather odd request.

" . . . My problem is this," he said after the usual preliminaries to asking a favor had been gone through. "I have a picture which I would like identified. It was taken over four years ago." That was a lie because he had taken it in his flat only two nights ago. " . . . and the subject's name and nationality are unknown. He was probably a top airline pilot or test pilot, so his picture should have appeared in the aviation journals at that time or earlier—anything later than four years ago is no good because he may have been killed or taken to chicken farming since

105

then. What I would like to know is whether one of your clipping agencies is capable of conducting a search of four-year-old and earlier journals, home and foreign, for someone whose name and nationality I don't know but whose picture I do have. I would also like it done quickly, and very quietly."

There was a long pause, then Simpson said, "This one I'd better handle myself, Joe. Just send the picture . . . "

Suddenly Carson had a rush of second thoughts. But Pebbles, he told himself reassuringly, was only one of twelve thousand employees and Simpson was a very busy man. Even if he did more than glance at the photograph he would probably not recognize the man, anyway.

"Right away, and thanks," said Carson. He added, "I suppose you're curious to know why I—"

"Joe," said Simpson very seriously, "I have had a very hard three days. The people responsible for releasing the news about Tillotson will not, for some reason, furnish us with exact information on the type of plane he was flying or what he was supposed to be doing or, for that matter, where he was doing it. Nobody will say anything for the record and off the record they say they just don't know, and the buck has been passed around so often it has gone into orbit."

A deep sigh rustled into Simpson's mouth-piece and he went on, "Now some idiots are suggesting that it was a new and very hush-hush Hart-Ewing aircraft and we are trying to cover up. Printed insanity of this kind is highly contagious, so you will understand, Joe, that the only thing I am curious about is why I continue to work in this madhouse!"

Carson took another risk that night when he entered Daniels' office and dialed his own extension. He used the spare internal phone by the window and after dialing left the receiver off the hook. The internal telephone system worked off an automatic PBX and could not be tapped without considerable trouble and advance knowledge of the line being used.

When he arrived back at the main patrol office, Donovan said, "Your telephone has been ringing for nearly ten minutes, sir. A persistent cuss, whoever he is. I would have answered it for you but you locked your office door . . . "

"I was going home," said Carson, ostentatiously fishing for his keys, "then I remembered something I had to do . . . "

He closed the door firmly behind him, lifted the receiver and carried on half a conversation for a few minutes before placing it carefully on his blotter. Now all he had to do was act natural, pop in and out of his office occasionally to ask about duty rosters and to cadge coffee . . . and wait.

He had to wait until nearly eight-thirty.

The first sound he heard was a door opening. This was followed by footsteps, the murmur of at least three different conversations. One of them was loud enough for him to catch part of it . . .

"*. . . And now he is insisting on a more accurate fix. Eighteen point five and two hundred and fifteen miles per second, and now we have to compute for just over one thousand miles an hour—an hour, mind you!—as well. In miles per second that is a negligible distance. What do they carry reserve fuel for . . .*"

"*If the time and position are really accurate they would not need fuel at all, so he has a point. But is your one thousand and thirty-four corrected for launch latitude or is it equatorial . . . ?*"

Another voice was raised suddenly. It sounded like Daniels himself.

"*Settle down, please. This will be a short one, I hope—discussion only and no paperwork to worry about afterwards. Now that you've all had a chance to think about it, I would like to have your ideas on what it was that could cause a man like Wayne Tillotson to behave in the way he did prior to re-entry . . .*"

The voice had been reducing in volume as the other people in the room grew quiet until now Carson could no longer hear it clearly. Neither could he distinguish any of the replies. He jammed the receiver so tightly against his ear that it hurt while he pushed a finger into his other ear to deaden the sounds coming from the patrol office, but still he could not make out more than one word in six.

The telephone which he had left off the hook in Daniels' office was about seven yards from the conference table, and his problem might be additionally complicated by the fact that the speakers had their backs to the phone. It was a spare telephone, after all, in an inconspicuous corner and was rarely used since the geography of the room's desk, tables and filing cabinets had been changed a few months earlier—Carson would never have been able to get away with this trick otherwise.

He swore under his breath and strained even harder to listen. But whenever one of the voices was raised a little, a truck went past or a plane went snarling into the air or somebody in the outer office had a fit of coughing. Apparently he would only hear what was going on when somebody became excited or angry.

One man in particular was becoming very angry.

    ". . . at a loss to understand how you can be so cold-blooded about him! You showed more emotion over the guinea-pigs, dammit. They couldn't tell us what happened, but they were badly confused for weeks afterwards. Wayne did not have time to become de-confused, did he? He did not have time for anything except—"

    "He should not have overridden the automatic controls! He would have been all right otherwise . . ."

    "I know he wasn't supposed to, that he would have been landed safely if he hadn't, but he did. And we were expecting so much from this trip—a thinking, self-controlled, articulate man instead of a few confused guinea-pigs. Instead he . . ."

"He cried like a baby. At the end he cried like a baby with its night-clothes on fire . . . !"

"I am being deliberately unemotional in order to be constructive. I liked him as much as you did!"

"I agree with him, Steve—our grief should be private. And it does seem to be the software which is letting us down on this one. The effect works, but there are psychological, perhaps even philosophical, complications as well. We're breaking quite a few of the accepted natural laws with this space drive— Einstein, for one, would not have approved—and crime doesn't pay. From here to the orbit of Mars in the blink of an eye—faster than that because we can at least measure the blink of an eye! —must break something more than a speed record. The trouble is we don't know what law it is we're breaking or the punishment being meted out . . ."

Donovan came into the office at that moment to have a uniform requisition signed and to talk about the way pants were always wearing out before tunics. Carson, the phone pressed tightly to his ear, moved his hand towards the dial and stopped with one finger poised. He was trying desperately to listen with one ear and not listen to Donovan with the other. The strain must have shown on his face because the senior patrol officer gave him a worried look as he left.

Meanwhile in Daniels' office the argument, and the audibility, was dying away. Odd words and phrases rose from time to time from the background murmuring, but out of context they meant absolutely nothing. Carson found himself wishing for another argument to start so hard that his jaw ached, but it did not happen until nearly half an hour later when the meeting was beginning to break up.

He recognized the voice as that of the man who had objected to the apparently callous treatment of Tillotson's death.

" . . . some sort of recognition for what he did? As

109

it is he's just another pilot lost over the sea. Some kind of medal, perhaps . . . "

"What good would that do him? He has no living close relatives. That is why he was chosen . . ."

"And that is why we are using Pebbles. His mental problems are irrelevant when we have complete control. He won't be taking the long way back . . . "

"Wayne was against using Pebbles towards the end. He said that it wasn't fair that—"

"Where would we find another physically fit guinea-pig, without friends or relations to complain if something . . . peculiar . . . happened to him . . . ?"

"But he isn't a moron, you know. Wayne said that potentially he might be very bright . . . "

"I still say Wayne should get some kind of recognition . . . !"

There was a single, sharp crack of someone hitting the table with something hard and heavy, then silence. A few seconds later Carson heard a voice speaking not very quietly and, because it was the only voice, very clearly.

"Let's face it, gentlemen, Wayne is not going to be awarded a posthumus medal for gallantry or gain any other recognition. He did not want it when he was alive and I don't see him changing his mind now. This project is too secret for that. If we started agitating for medals for people the intelligence departments will begin taking an interest. They may discover that we are working on something that is potentially much more than a space drive which can, once we get rid of the unwanted side-effects, open up the stars to humanity. They will see applications much nearer home.

"Our present master is scared stiff by what we have here. That is why he allows these peculiar security arrangements. He wants us to succeed before his more warlike colleagues realize that we have a weapon which makes early warning systems and anti-

missile missiles obsolete. They would cover us with so much security that the other side could not help but notice it, and start digging. Before we knew it there would be another arms race going on, and this one would be so expensive that it would wreck both our economies—I've calculated the cost of moving our entire nuclear arsenal into space and I know.

"With the sort of control and guidance we are beginning to achieve we could place a bomb of any desired megatonnage in any cellar of any house in any city in the world, and there would be no possible way of stopping it because it would arrive before—"

"We've been over this before, sir! But you're forgetting that there may be people on the other side who feel as we do . . . !"

"I don't doubt it. But like us they are outnumbered by people who want to look hours instead of years ahead.

"Which brings us back to Pebbles. How far are we going to go with him? We have to bear in mind, of course, that he will not be in control at any point. He will not even be allowed to press the return button. By rights he should be shot full of pain-killers, supportive medication, psychological buffers, and anything else which would enable him to survive whatever it was that got Tillotson and still leave him in a condition to talk about it afterwards. Unfortunately, we lack specialist advice on that subject and for security reasons cannot ask for it.

"I suggest using the long-range boosters to a spatial equivalent of four hours . . ."

Carson lost them for several minutes because they all began talking at once. They were still talking over the sounds of chairs being pushed back as the meeting broke up. When the last few men were leaving the office some-one—it sounded like the man who had wanted recognition for Tillotson—said something which left Carson feeling completely confused.

" . . . *And he shouldn't forget that it is twenty-eight million, five hundred and twelve thousand-odd miles away, and right now tomorrow is too far . . .*"

Only half a mile away, a door slammed.

Chapter 15

For her own sake, Carson had not wanted Jean Marshall to become too deeply involved. Now that he had some idea of the tremendous importance of the project, he felt even more worried about bringing her in on it. But he had to have specialist assistance to evaluate and advise him on the Pebbles material. He needed her help and, as her visits to the flat became more frequent, he found that he needed —or at least badly wanted—her.

Those were the reasons why, when he had finished telling her about the meeting in Daniels' office, he slipped his arm around her waist and said, "I'm beginning to worry about you. Neither of us has any business knowing this stuff. I don't want to get you shot."

"We can share the last cigarette," she said, removing his hand. "You did say that we had a lot of work to get through tonight . . . ?"

"I could say something ponderous and unoriginal," he replied, turning towards the tape-recorder, "about all work and no play . . . "

He was trying to conceal his anger and disappointment but not, he suspected, doing a very good job of it.

"And I could say something about workmates not necessarily being playmates," Jean replied coldly. "You don't have to worry about involving me in this thing. It . . . I

113

can hardly believe how big it is, but I would not have missed being involved in it for anything. And for your professional handling of the investigation I have nothing but admiration, but as a person I don't even know if I like you, Joe."

"But . . . "

"You see, I don't like what we are doing. It's shameful. And I can't make up my mind whether you're trying to help Pebbles or crucify him."

"That," said Carson, jabbing hard on the play-back button, "makes two of us . . . "

For a long time neither spoke. He was playing back the tape through matched speakers, with the volume turned well up but not uncomfortably loud. Each footfall, click of door lock and sound of body against upholstery came in sharp and clear, as did every word and even the breaths between words.

Carson could not help contrasting this conversation with the one he had strained to hear in Daniels' office. Here every nuance and emotional overtone was plain and, if it was not quite plain enough the first time it could be re-run until it was. During the first twenty minutes or so, while Carson writhed inwardly at the still strange sound of his own voice, nothing of importance was said. But then they came to the section where Carson had begun questioning Pebbles about his mental state and early memories . . .

" . . . You say it was hard to think in those days, John. Can you remember what it was like exactly? Were you aware that you should have been quicker on the uptake?"

"Yes, I can remember some of it. Everybody seemed to talk gibberish. I didn't know it was gibberish then because I didn't know anything at all, but I still felt that it was gibberish. Maybe it was because people spoke differently when I was dreaming. In my dreams I almost understood what they said, but I didn't dream often—my mind was too empty. The peculiar thing was that I knew it was empty and that

frightened me badly. Do you understand, Joe? There wasn't enough in my mind to dream with. I . . . I seem to remember waking up from nightmares in the very early days because nothing, nothing at all, was going to happen. Joe, maybe I do need a psychiatrist . . . "

"You would only need a psychiatrist if your condition was getting worse, and even you must admit that mentally you have been steadily improving. But dreaming is important to health. Do you dream now, and if so, what happens in them? And, John, there is no need to tell me about sex fantasies or anything in that area . . . "

"Tact," said Carson.
"Cold feet, you mean," said Jean.

" . . . quite a lot these nights and it scares me, Joe. The people in the dreams talk and show me books printed in the same gibberish I talk and read every day—you see, I still have this peculiar feeling that everything we're saying is gibberish. Sometimes, not often, the dream people talk a different gibberish which I understand just as well. When this happens I get really afraid and wake up and . . . and the lady who owns the house is starting to get angry because I shout and scream. You see, the frightening thing about these other people, the ones who speak this different, familiar gibberish, is that they look like ordinary people but they aren't. There is something different about them and about me . . . "

"Lots of people believe they're different. The delusion that one is in reality of noble blood, kidnapped from the palace as a very young baby, that sort of thing, is fairly common. Quite normal people have daydreams about it, but rarely nightmares. It's nothing to worry about. These people, these different people, do they call you 'Sir' or 'General' or 'Your Majesty' . . . ?"

115

"Don't laugh, Joe. It . . . it's getting so bad I'm afraid to go to sleep."

"I'm sorry. But what exactly are you afraid of? Are these . . . different . . . people trying to hurt you?"

"I don't know. They aren't trying to hurt me but they did. They seem to like me, even respect me, but I'm sure they mean to do something terrible to me. Some of them call me 'sir,' I think, but they are still going to wipe me out. I don't know how because I wake up yelling before I can find out."

"John, you said that they aren't trying to hurt you but they did. What exactly did they do?"

"They didn't do anything. But one of these nights they will."

"I see. You got your tenses mixed up a little just then, but no matter. What is it that you're afraid they'll do? Torture you? Subject you to a series of painful tests, medical or psychological, perhaps? Is there any special phobia you have, something which makes you particularly afraid? These nightmares are your subconscious trying to tell you about it. Did someone nearly kill you when you were a child . . . But, then, you can't remember your childhood . . ."

"I don't think they killed me—will kill me, I'm sure that it was worse than that . . ."

"A fate worse than death, eh? But I refuse to believe that your subconscious could take things that literally . . . !"

"The rest of it is pretty repetitious," Carson said as he pressed the Hold button, "but then if it was full of Grade A Freudian slips I probably wouldn't even notice. You can hear it all later, of course. Right now I'd like to know what you think so far?"

"There isn't much that you wouldn't notice," she said, "and false modesty doesn't become you."

Carson tried not to lose his temper. He said, "Why do

you always try to start a fight? You're beginning to analyze the wrong patient, Jean . . . "

"Very well," she broke in, "I'll stick to the other one. In my professional opinion John Pebbles is a very frightened man. At the moment he does not know what exactly it is that is frightening him. I would say that this is because the person or thing or event which is frightening him has not yet appeared or happened. It is possible, even highly probable, that he is only beginning to consciously realize that something is threatening him—but his subconscious is screaming blue murder! Are they really planning a dangerous mission for him and beginning, perhaps, to hint at what the risks might be?"

"He is going to be, or he may already have been, asked to do something very risky indeed," Carson said. "Wayne Tillotson got killed doing it. But I'm pretty sure that they haven't told him about the risks."

"Then he is beginning to suspect," she said seriously, "that his friends aren't really his friends. He may even be beginning to suspect you, Joe. And don't shake your head —you've admitted that your suspicions have caused a change of feeling towards him and he is sensitive, as sensitive as a child."

Carson leaned forward to rewind the tape, for no other reason than to avoid her eyes while he was speaking. He was beginning to feel like something that had crawled from under a damp stone, and he was afraid that her expression would show that she agreed with him.

He said, "It's your whole theory I'm shaking my head at. It's a good theory, full of common sense and it seems to fit all the facts. But just suppose that your theory is completely wrong and you were asked to think of one a little bit far-fetched, ridiculous even . . . ?"

"How ridiculous would you like it to be?" She paused, then added drily, "Perhaps you could tell me about your own ridiculous theory and give me some sort of guide."

"I don't have enough information to form a theory," Carson said angrily. "I need the sort of data which is not found in psychological texts and periodicals for interested laymen like myself, but reports of experimental and probably dangerous work, so far as the patients would be concerned. It might be the psychological equivalent of nerve gas, the kind of thing that is hinted at or mentioned speculatively in the more restricted journals. New methods of brainwashing, drug-reinforced hypnotic techniques, that sort of thing. The truth is that I'm not quite sure what sort of information I'm looking for."

"I see," she said.

Carson kept his eyes on the tape deck while the silence began to drag. Finally he said, "Some things go out of fashion faster than others. Take patriotism, for instance. The out-and-out, 'my country-right-or-wrong' type of patriot is very rare these days—which is a good thing, because fanaticism of any kind is not a good thing. In its place we have intelligent self-interest. This is much better, I suppose, than blind patriotism. But self-interest and self-ishness are synonymous so far as I'm concerned—I mean, who ever heard of intelligent self-interest winning someone the Congressional Medal or the Victoria Cross?"

It was a purely rhetorical question so he did not wait for an answer. "Something more than intelligent self-interest motivates the feelings of parents and children, relatives and friends, for each other. A self-interested and really intelligent man could find lots of ways of not doing anything but enjoy himself all his life by using the mental shortcomings or sympathy or generosity or love of those around him. But very few people live this way. They prefer to work because, in my opinion, they feel that they owe *something* to the people and country where they were born —even though they disagree with the politics of the government in power, and insist that the Russians or the Japanese manage things so much better, and complain bitterly about the proportion of their income tax which goes to defense and generally carry on as if they were on the verge of rebellion. I'm over-simplifying, but do you see what I mean?"

He was still staring at the recorder, his right index finger moving around the dimpled top of the Hold button.

"I can see that you have a perhaps juvenile hankering for the days of cavalry charges and deeds of derring-do, but you are too intelligent to ignore the spitted and dismembered people, disembowelled horses and the other gory by-products of that romantic age. I can also see you trying hard to put up very good reasons for doing something which you yourself feel is very wrong, and that the fact that you are an open-eyed patriot is keeping you from taking the easy way out. Or am I analyzing the wrong patient again?"

"You are," said Carson.

"Maybe the reason," she said, in a surprisingly gentle tone, "is that you are supplying me with more material on Joe Carson than on John Pebbles."

"I was simply trying to make the point," said Carson, "that it is possible to like a man or love a girl and still feel angry because he or she is something different."

"All right, Joe. But you started to tell me about a ridiculous theory you had. Maybe you should stick to that point instead of trying to make another one . . . "

They were both sitting tense and upright on a couch which was designed to topple the occupants backwards into its deep, soft upholstery and enfold them so comfortably that they would feel it impossible to climb out again without the help of ropes. The muscular strain involved in fighting that seductive piece of furniture was considerable. Carson flopped back and tried to relax mentally as well as physically before he spoke.

"Very well. My ridiculous theory is that Dreamy Daniels is heading a Most Secret project which requires guinea-pigs with a high degree of flying aptitude and no close relatives or friends. John Pebbles is a natural choice —simpleminded in practically everything other than aeronautics, impressionable, nobody really to care what happens to him and, with his background, completely above suspicion so far as the security of the project is concerned.

"Someone has been very clever with their John Pebbles," Carson continued. "He or they have displayed con-

119

siderable finesse by so arranging things that it has been project men who have actually invited him in instead of putting the spy to the trouble and risk of penetrating project security. They have been even cleverer by sending in an agent whose cover cannot possibly be blown because he does not even know that he *is* a spy, and won't until they contact him and play back the organic tape-recorder that is John Pebbles' mind."

He paused, waiting for a reaction which did not come, then went on, "The way I see it, John Pebbles had a normal childhood. He was fit and intelligent and probably wanted to be a pilot when he grew up, and eventually he did. I would say that flying was probably the biggest thing in his life, that he really loved being a pilot and that he was certainly one of their best men—a top-level test pilot, at least, possibly a potential or actual cosmonaut.

"Then a little over four years ago someone wiped his memory clean . . .

"They had left him on a beach before first light, at a spot where rocky outcroppings made it difficult and uncomfortable for him to crawl into the sea and drown. There was not much risk of his dying from exposure—they could not, of course, dress him because of the risk of the clothing being traced—since they would have already been aware of the habits of the Clinic personnel.

"The result was that a mature, physically fit and highly trained man with the mind of a new-born baby was brought to the Clinic and the process of re-eductaion was begun. John Pebbles learned fast because, apart from the fact that it was completely empty, there was nothing at all wrong with his mind.

"And sometimes, when the wind was in the right quarter, aircraft from the club would slide in over the hospital grounds on finals . . .

" . . . It was all carefully planned from the very beginning," Carson went on angrily. "His memory was wiped clean, but his training and aptitudes remained to nag at his subconscious and gradually break the conditioning

120

which had made him forget. But they must have planned even this as well . . ."

"There's no need to shout, Joe."

" . . . Dr. Morris and Nurse Sampson were right when they thought he might be an amnesia victim," Carson went on in a calmer tone. "He was the most complete amnesia case they are ever likely to meet! And the cure for amnesia is to surround the patient with familiar people, places and things, remember. The trips to the club airfield was the begiinning of his 'cure' and the process accelerated rapidly when he joined Hart-Ewing—familiar surroundings, you see. But the familiar faces and spoken or written language he did not have, so he had to learn to read and write from scratch.

"But now his virtual return to normal in the aviation area is causing the rest of the conditioning to crack. He's beginning to dream about people talking to him in another language and have nightmares because he has begun to remember what it was they were going to do to him—destroy his memory! Very soon he will remember who he is and which country he belongs to. He will probably feel grateful to us and will not want to pass on all the very valuable information he has absorbed to his own people, and for a while he will be very confused and unhappy and not quite sane. So if his own people are going to finish this job as cold-bloodedly as they began it, they may send someone to contact him and secure his knowledge before he recovers his memory completely.

"I would say," Carson ended grimly, "that the contact could occur any day now."

Jean Marshall was silent for a moment, then she said quietly, "Everything you've said is possible, Joe, if a little melodramatic. But what are you going to do? Denounce him?"

Carson shook his head. "It's what I should do. Not that they would shoot him—that is very rarely done these days. But they would subject him to continuous and intensive interrogation, most of it in his own language. His memory would come back and he would realize that he was in

121

fact the spy that they accused him of being, and that there was nothing he could do about it.

"I would hate for anything like that to happen to him," he went on, "because he is innocent—at least, he is at the moment. And even if I did decide to turn him in and put my country's security above personal feelings, it is still not that simple.

"You must remember that the project is secret," Carson continued, "*really* secret. I am not supposed to know that it exists and can therefore expect serious trouble if I reveal a threat to something which is not supposed to exist. You could expect serious trouble, too, because I did not keep my knowledge of it to myself. There is also the fact that this penetration was planned five or more years ago at a time when the project was just getting under way. This means that the project already may have contained someone sympathetic to the other side, in which case why should they go to all the trouble of setting up the Pebbles operation—they already *knew* about the project! You see, even now I could be entirely wrong about John Pebbles . . . "

"But what *are* you going to do, Joe?"

She was still sitting upright on the edge of the couch, looking straight ahead so that all he could see was the line of her cheek, jaw and neck which showed as a complex pink curve against the dark bookcases on the other side of the room. One earlobe showed below the sweep of rich auburn hair, a very nice earlobe but not exactly expressive.

Why did she have to fight with him over Pebbles all the time? Surely he was doing enough fighting with himself over the man.

He said, "I don't know what to do, Jean. The project is too important for me to forget it and do nothing. I think that we should continue working on him until *we* find out who and what he is. Is it possible to cure or de-condition him before his own people make contact?"

Still she did not look at him. "And if we did bring back his memory, then what?"

122

"Then I'll have the slightly comforting knowledge that he as well as we knew that he was a spy. I would find out a lot more about the project. I might not have to turn him in after all, if he was angry enough at his own people for what they did to him and, of course, grateful enough to us. If I did denounce him we might find ourselves locked away for the rest of our lives or until the project was declassified, a very long time in either event. I would also get some idea of the methods used by these people to produce a Pebbles-type agent so that we would be on the lookout for them in the future.

"I would also," he ended worriedly, "get rid of this very strong feeling I have that this business is even more important and complex than it looks at the moment . . . "

He broke off as Jean relaxed and lay back in the couch beside him. Her expression, when she looked at him, was sympathetic but not at all clinical.

"Let's have the tape again," she said, "but later . . . "

Chapter 16

It was a cold, wet, blustery Sunday afternoon. The dull gray breakers thumped steadily against the rocky beach, sending up thick clouds of spray to join the slightly thinner curtain of falling rain. As they picked their way over the rocks the drops rattled against their raincoats like hail, and the wind was a great soft pillow pushing against their faces and muffling everything they said.

"Here," said Nurse Sampson, stopping suddenly and pointing. Despite her heavy coat, the cold had made her face closer to gray than chocolate brown. "You were curled up behind this rock when I found you. But can you remember anything before that time, anything at all, John?"

"I seem to remember you finding me," Pebbles replied, "although at the time I was too stupid to know what it was I was remembering. Before that . . . " he stared hard at the dark, wet sand and dripping rock for several minutes, then went on, "Water. I can remember being in the water, swallowing some of it and being frightened. Nothing else, I'm afraid . . . "

"You might have accidentally crawled into the water," said Jean Marshall, "or crawled *out* of it. Can you remember being on any kind of boat?"

A submarine, perhaps? Carson added, but under his

124

breath. They were getting so very close to the beginning now. Surely the end of the mystery was in sight.

"You didn't have any clothes on," Jean went on, when Pebbles had shaken his head. "Can you remember anyone taking them off? Or you taking them off or struggling out of them because you were in the water and could not swim so well with them on? You *can* swim, John?"

"Yes," said Pebbles. "I always could. When Nurse Sampson started to teach me at the Clinic's pool she said that she didn't have to, that I could swim very well. I . . . I did it without thinking. I'm sorry, I can't remember getting undressed."

"Betty," said Jean, turning to the nurse, "are you sure there was no clothing near him, or marks on his body of clothing recently worn? I'm thinking of the indentations left by, say, a tight belt or tight sock tops or even a wristwatch. You see, he was in such good physical condition—whoever it was who had been taking care of him had done such a good job of it—that the sheer cruelty of leaving him without clothing before dawn on a beach at that time of year just doesn't fit. Do you see what I'm getting at? Why take away his clothes?"

They didn't want to give us the name of his tailor, thought Carson with silent cynicism. There was no need for him to speak when Jean was asking all the right questions.

"I didn't see any clothing and with John in that condition I didn't waste very much time looking," Betty Sampson said sharply. Perhaps she was irritated by what she thought was an implied criticism, or it might simply have been the cold making her tense. The smooth chocolate skin of her face was roughened by goosebumps, and when she spoke again the hissing rain reinforced the sibilants in her words, making her sound like a stage Oriental.

"Besides, the marks made by clothing, even tight clothing, fade in a few hours. And we examined him very closely—we thought he might be a drug addict, you see, or a diabetic in hypoglycemic shock, or maybe an epileptic." She looked an apology at Pebbles for referring to him

125

so often in the third person, then went on, "His arms showed a number of fairly recent punctures—they could have been made anything from a week to three weeks earlier—but blood tests showed no residual traces of drugs, or anything unusual, in his bloodstream . . . "

And so it went on, the two girls questioning and Pebbles trying hard and hiding nothing but not helping at all. Carson's impatience and anger were growing until he felt almost a pain. A few days ago he had told Jean that Pebbles was innocent—as innocent as an unfused bomb—and that he should be treated gently and de-conditioned by Jean and himself rather than be interrogated by one of the intelligence agencies. Carson was beginning to wonder if he had said those things just to avoid sounding like a louse.

But the cold-blooded, callous way that John Pebbles had been used, how the Clinic and Mrs. Kirk had been used to give him an unbreakable cover, how Hart-Ewing and Dreamy Daniels had been used and manipulated, made him angry in a way he had never been angry before. He was a little like Bill Savage, he supposed, in that he preferred to think of men as people instead of useful or potentially useful things. This thing called Pebbles could be very useful to Carson as well as to its masters and after all, what did a bomb casing care about a few dents and scratches when its fate was to be blown to pieces, anyway?

He found himself looking up at the dark, shredded clouds while raindrops scored near-misses on his eyes, imagining the clean, cold rain and spray rotten with radioactivity and the clear, still air above them empty of aircraft and nobody on the Moon or Mars or on the extrasolar planets beyond, which were now almost within reach. A weapon against which there was absolutely no protection was bad because the only deterrent was to use it first.

This was too big a thing for one man's feelings to be given any weight, much too big for it to be important whether a certain doctor thought Carson a louse or even whether he thought the same himself . . .

Carson became aware that Jean was talking to him. He said, "I'm sorry, I was thinking. Let's go back to the car.

The club isn't far from here and we can all get a nice, hot lunch ... "

It was what you said that was important to most people, not what you thought. Carson was thinking that starting tomorrow he was going to get very tough with John Pebbles.

But next day Pebbles was gone. Despite a large number of carefully offhand inquiries, Carson could not find out why or where. He did not show on the following two days, either. Carson began to wonder if he had already been contacted and was in the process of being de-conditioned, if one of his own people had beaten him to the punch. He thought of the language tuition tapes he had just bought that were waiting for Pebbles' next visit to the flat.

Jean Marshall had not wanted him to experiment with the language records too soon. Rushing things like this, she had insisted, might give rise to all sorts of emotional disturbances in their patient, especially if Carson's theory was correct.

She seemed to think that they had all the time in the world.

On the fourth day of Pebbles' absence Carson took an afternoon off and spent it going through the local newspaper files around the date of Pebbles' discovery on the beach. He found out nothing beyond the fact that the area had been covered by a late-autumn fog around that time, and nobody had reported seeing small boats, submarines or even UFOs. He wondered if the plastic material Nurse Sampson had mentioned, and which she had insisted was not rubber dinghy material, was some kind of parachute.

He had just about decided that there was nothing he could do until Pebbles returned when, early on the fifth day, Simpson in Publicity rang to say that he had something for him.

It turned out to be a large envelope full of magazine clippings. Carson took them back to his office to examine them at leisure, not expecting very much from them, but ten minutes later he was on the phone to Simpson.

"Of course I'll help you, if I can," said the publicity

man. "But your voice sounds funny, Joe—have you a sore throat or is this a bad line . . . ?"

Carson tried to contain his excitement and lower the pitch of his voice as he gave the title, page and date of the magazine and added, "I'm very interested in one of the pictures. It shows a group of pilots surrounded by inset pictures of, I think, the aircraft they fly. But the caption does not give the names of the individual pilots. Is there any way of finding out who they are?"

Simpson was silent for a moment, then said, "I'm not sure, Joe. I recognize the magazine and date, of course —it was an issue devoted to one of the big international aerospace shows which was held the preceding month. Companies and even Government information agencies buy space on these occasions and try to place as much editorial material as possible—it's a matter of national prestige, you see. The item you're interested in sounds like a puff about the pilots taking part in that country's flying display.

"That particular magazine is a very small one," Simpson went on, "so I would think that the only way you would have of finding out the pilots' names would be to scan the larger magazines published at the same time. They would also have covered the show and might possibly have used the same picture with a more detailed caption."

"Could you . . . " began Carson.

"I could try, Joe, but you could probably do the job quicker and easier yourself by calling in on Ben Mitchell at the library. He keeps bound volumes of all the principal aviation magazines back to the Wright brothers. You have the date, now, so it is just a matter of checking through the different magazine files for that period . . . "

On the way to the technical library he called in at Engineering Test to check whether Pebbles had returned or not. He had not, but Daniels was there ostentatiously displaying no interest in the crated and supposedly substandard module which was being loaded on to an articulated truck belonging to a local transport company. To be junk, Carson thought, the module was being very carefully handled.

The presence of God, sometimes known as the Chief of Design, was making everyone appear unusually industrious and not disposed towards idle conversation. Even Donovan, who was standing beside the cab with the driver and whose duty it was to see that non-company transport did not take short cuts between parked aircraft and risk knocking off a tail or wing-tip, was watching Daniels out of the corner of his eye and had very little time for his own chief.

Carson went to the nearest outside telephone and called Jean Marshall. She was having a day off at home in lieu of a spell of night duty worked the preceding week. When she answered he said, "Jean, how would you like to follow a truck . . . ?"

A little later as he was entering the building which housed the technical library, Carson called at the patrol office to lay some groundwork for his probable presence in the library later that night. He discovered that there would be a meeting in Daniels' office at seven-thirty that evening.

He *knew* that it was going to be an important one . . .

In the library he used the outside phone to call Jean again and was lucky enough to catch her before she left. There was nobody within earshot but he avoided being specific—this was not, after all, an automatic, unmanned exchange—as he asked her if she would not mind letting herself into the flat and taking a call he was expecting sometime after seven o'clock. She could amuse herself with the tape-recorder until he arrived later. He hoped she would be back in time to do this because it was a very important call . . .

He could always eavesdrop on the meeting from his office as he had done the last time. But this meeting, he felt sure, was going to be a very important one and he did not want his eavesdropping to be interrupted by Donovan or one of the other patrolmen wanting to know if they could help him or make coffee. This way he could use the

129

recorder attachment for telephone calls and later go over the tape of the meeting as often as he liked, and if the level of conversation dropped too low he could simply crank up the volume—if he was lucky, that was, and Jean returned from checking on the truck in time.

Carson felt lucky. Everything seemed to be going his way today.

He was lucky again in the library. Carson found the information he needed in just under two hours although he did not, of course, tell Ben Mitchell that. Instead he talked to the technical librarian about a series of articles he hoped to do someday on the subject of second-generation space flight, pointing up the fact that recent advances in the art were making it unnecessary for astronauts to be supermen and that the way was opening for purely commercial, or even pleasure, trips to the Moon and planets.

Perhaps he overdid it a little, but Mitchell did not seem to think it strange that a security officer should want to write as a hobby, but he professed mild surprise that it was not spy stories. The librarian did not mind how late Carson stayed researching, but he reminded him that it was against regulations to take books and technical material off company limits. In the meantime Mitchell said that he would get photo-copies of the pages and illustrations Carson was most interested in and let him have them in about twenty minutes.

He was thinking of those pages as he let himself into Daniels' office a little after seven o'clock. They had shown the picture in his clipping enlarged, reduced and in one case chopped to show only the man he was interested in plus two of his companions, and they had also named names. The photographs would lose detail in the copying process, which was meant to reproduce text rather than half-tones, but the face was recognizable and it was the name that was important.

The name was not Pebbles.

This time he went to the external telephone on the inconspicuous corner table. At this time there were no operators on the board and Daniels, being an important man in the company, had a private night line to his office. A little self-consciously Carson used his handkerchief to lift the receiver and the end of his ball-point to dial.

He heard the phone in his flat ringing and go on ringing. Jean had not arrived. His luck was beginning to change.

Carson laid down the receiver and walked around the large office. The ringing signal could be clearly heard everywhere, so he could not simply leave it as it was while he drove back to the flat and lifted his own receiver. That left him with no alternative but to eavesdrop from his office via the internal phone, except that he had not locked his office so that no matter how fast he drove down there he would be too late to stop one of the patrolmen lifting his receiver and replacing it when nobody spoke. And on the internal automatic PBX that would break the connection.

It was now seven-fifteen. An early arriver for the meeting might turn up at any minute.

Suddenly the burring from the receiver stopped. Carson ran to the table and picked it up. "Jean, I haven't much time . . . " he began.

"Joe, I followed the truck to the freight terminal," she said excitedly, ignoring him. "The driver left it there, among hundreds of others, just like it, and I drove away and came back again every time someone looked as if they might ask me what I was doing there. About an hour ago another front end drove up and hooked on to the trailer. There were two men in the cab, both in service denims; the vehicle was painted olive drab with military serial numbers in white. They threw a green tarpaulin over the crate and trailer name panel and drove away. With the olive drab horse and tarp, its own mother would not have recognized the load.

"And Joe," she rushed on, "they came back here! They showed some papers at the airfield gate, drove through and on to that old C-5A that arrived this morning, which took off a few minutes later. Somebody thinks a lot of our scrapped components, Joe . . . "

131

"Yes, yes," said Carson, practically sweating with impatience. She sounded so excited and pleased with herself. He should compliment her but there was no time. He went on, "Jean, listen carefully. Set up to record through the phone. Try not to make any noise while you're doing it, and afterwards don't cough or sneeze or make any noise whatever unless you go into the other room. Any noise you make at that end might be picked up by the receiver here loudly enough to be noticed by someone in this room. And Jean, leave the flat door ajar so's I won't have to make a noise with the doorbell. Got all that?"

"Yes, Joe."

"Good, I'm leaving now . . . "

He walked slowly past the patrol office, trying so hard not to run that he felt that he would fall on his face, and across to the car. As he moved away, Daniels pulled in.

Chapter 17

When he tiptoed into the flat half an hour later his telephone receiver was in its rest, the tape-recorder was switched off and loud cooking noises were coming from the kitchen. His disappointment was like a physical blow.

"What *happened* . . . !"

"I'm not sure," said Jean over her shoulder. "We'll probably find out during the playback. All I know is that they hung up on us about three minutes ago. I haven't had anything to eat since taking off after that truck. Are you hungry?"

A little later they took their trays into the lounge beside the recorder and ate as they listened. They listened so intently that when a fork scraped a plate or a cup clinked softly against a saucer they practically snarled at each other to be quiet.

But for the first ten minutes or so there was nothing but a hissing, over-amplified silence. Then there was the sound of approaching footsteps, of a door opening and closing several times and the rhubarbing of three or four conversations going on at once, and finally one voice louder than the others . . .

"Settle down, please. George, sit in a chair and not on the edge of my desk—this will be a long ses-

sion, believe me. Now, let's get on with it. Parsons?"

"No trace of the vehicle or Tillotson. The search was thorough even though they thought they were helping me look for an important instrument package. Dammit, why is it that a stupid machine can make the minus trip and not a man . . . ?"

"A stupid man might make it . . ."

"Pebbles isn't stupid, just innocent. But what does that make us . . . ?"

"All right, all right, guilty. But he's quite happy about it all. There was no need to tell him that he is to make a minus trip like Tillotson because he is unlikely to run into the same trouble—"

"But we don't know what the trouble was, so how . . . ?"

"Because we are controlling everything from the ground. He is an overgrown child and he's living the dream that most children—and a lot of adults, too —have these days. He'll be in space, a real live astronaut, but without the responsibilities of having to maneuver his vehicle or reposition it for re-entry or do anything at all . . . What the blazes do you mean by jumping up like that . . . !"

"It's my car! I've just remembered that it's giving trouble again, sir. Can I take a minute to ring the mechanic I know in Transport to have a look at it during the meeting? It could be important to have it checked before our trip tomorrow . . ."

"Your blasted car, at a time like this! You should . . . ah . . . Oh, well, use my phone and be quick about it."

"Thank you, sir. Sorry, fellows . . . Hello, Transport? Donaldson here. It's happened again, I'm afraid. Do you think you could come along and have a look at it? That's very good of you. About fifteen minutes. Thank you . . ."

Carson refilled his coffee cup and said, "I didn't know Bill Donaldson had such influence. Getting a Transport mechanic to check out a private car—during night shift, too—is quite a trick . . . "

"Settle down, Bill. Stop worrying about it, there's probably a very simple explanation. Dammit, I suppose we won't get any constructive thinking out of you, or anyone else, until you know what is wrong with that blasted scrap-heap . . . !"

"Sir! You are speaking of the woman I love . . . !"

"Dreamy Daniels seems to have mellowed with age," Carson remarked. "This is an important meeting. I would have expected him to stamp hard on anyone who dared mention private troubles like sick relatives or cars. It doesn't sound right, somehow. I wonder what could have happened to . . . "

He began by wondering, but as the aimless chitchat continued Carson began to feel a little anxious. He thought back on the conversation they had already heard—useless, inconsequential conversation which had, perhaps, sounded just a little bit forced—searching for possible double meanings.

He found them.

"Joe," said Jean sharply, "what's the matter with you?"

His anxiety had built up rapidly to a fear that was close to panic. His mouth was too dry to speak. Before he could reply the tape-recorder made the sounds of a door being knocked and opened and the negative sound of a sudden silence falling in Daniels' office.

"I've traced the fault, Mr. Donaldson," said a new but oddly familiar voice. *"No need to worry about it anymore. Good-night, sir."*

"Good-night, and . . . and thank you. I must say that was quick—Hey, Bob! Your girl has left her phone off the hook again. I'll rep–"

The recording ended abruptly at that point. Jean said, "'What *is* the matter with you, Joe? Why are you looking at me like that . . . ?"

"Nothing," said Carson harshly, "except for a belated rush of brains to the head. Get your coat and things, Jean, and leave at once. Make sure you don't forget the scarf you left behind last week, or gloves or anything belonging to you. If anyone asks, and somebody surely will, you've spoken to me only during working hours. Stick to that story no matter what. Now get going! Walk home or catch a taxi—but don't ring one from here, there isn't time. I'll explain tomorrow at lunch, if I can. You must get out of here quickly before—"

He broke off suddenly as the realization came that she was staring, not at him, but at someone behind him. Carson swung around.

He was not really surprised to see Donovan standing there.

"I'd prefer for you both to sit just where you are," said Donovan quietly. "Don't move. Don't even talk . . ."

Donovan was capless, his topcoat collar turned up to hide the collar of his tunic and both hands were in his pockets. One of the pockets, indeed the whole coat on that side, was pulled off balance and deformed by what could have been a length of pipe carried horizontally in the pocket. Carson thought of the movie equivalent of this scene where the baddie's gun made a barely perceptible bulge in a coat which had been tailored with barely perceptible bulges in mind. He wanted suddenly to laugh, but then he reminded himself that Donovan's pocket would have concealed the weapon from passers-by when it was being carried vertically, that it became obvious only when it was being leveled, and that to be as obvious as this one was it had to be a very large caliber weapon fitted with a silencer.

"This looks bad, Donovan," he said, trying to keep his voice from squeaking, "but it isn't as bad as it looks. We were eavesdropping on that meeting—I've done it once before on the internal phone which, unlike this one, can't be traced from the other end. That was the only risk I took and you were right on to it . . . But the point I'm trying to make is that we are concerned over the security of your project, too. We are on *your* side . . . "

It was not so much that Donovan was not believing him; the other man looked as if he just did not care one way or the other. Carson doubted if he was even listening.

"For God's sake take that thing out of your pocket!" Jean burst out. More quietly she added, "You look ridiculous."

Too quickly for them to have done anything, even if they had considered doing it, he had the thing out of his pocket and leveled at them again. It looked as if it would stop an elephant.

"I don't want anyone to think," said Donovan, "that I was pointing a stiffened index finger at them."

This was much better, Carson thought. He laughed without overdoing it and said, "Dr. Marshall is involved in this because I needed professional advice—about a suspect, that is, not for myself. My own interest in the project stems from the fact that as the company's chief security officer I considered it my job to protect this project even if the project had no official classification and only a few people inside the company knew it existed— the security officer not being one of them.

"Maybe I was being over-conscientious," Carson went on quickly, "but a security man is, well, a security man. When my suspicions were first aroused—by small, apparently unimportant and senseless things like irregularities in accounting, planning errors which weren't caught until they had reached the very top and small, carefully set bonfires which were intended to burn more than waste paper—I began to dig. Gradually I began to turn up more and more information on this project that never was. A lot of it was guesswork, deduction on very slim evidence, but when I began to realize how big it was, that it involved no less than—"

"If you don't stop talking," said Donovan, "I'll kill you now."

For a long time nobody spoke. Donovan's eyes kept flicking to one side and back to them again, like a spectator watching a tennis match from one side of the court. There could be no doubt that he meant what he said but not, Carson hoped, exactly what he said. It was the subject, not talking itself, which was forbidden.

"You don't have to worry about an accomplice skulking in the bedroom or kitchen," Carson said. "There are only the two of us. But I don't suppose you believe that, either. And as for the project, we have a right to have our explanation heard and I should have thought you would be curious enough to—"

"He isn't curious, Joe," Jean broke in, and edge of desperation tinging the clinical calm of her voice. "He isn't really listening to you. He doesn't care what you say . . . "

"That's right, Doctor," said Donovan. "And you, Mr. Carson, have no right to an explanation or anything else. But to save you wasting your breath and because I'm in a hurry to settle this business, I'll explain very briefly. I am solely responsible for the security of a very important project, perhaps the most important project the world has ever known. That is all I have been told and that is all I need or want to know. The project consists of the people —not very many—who are actively engaged on it and one watchdog, me, to advise on security matters and to act when and where indicated. Project activities take place in the open alongside the normal day-to-day work of the departments concerned. Paperwork originates, has very limited circulation, and is destroyed without going outside. There is no code name, no classification grading, nothing known about it outside except for a remembered but not recorded conversation with someone very high in the administration which took place about five years ago. You see, Mr. Daniels thought that naming and classifying the project would attract attention to it, first from the various security organizations engaged in protecting it and later, as the inevitable leaks occurred, from the other side. Mr. Daniels went right to the top and his project was so important that the top man agreed to throw away the rules."

"I was *sure* something like that had happened..." began Carson.

"And I'm really not listening to you," Donovan went on patiently, "because when something like this happens my job is not very pleasant, and for reasons which you will understand shortly I cannot afford to become emotionally involved."

Carson looked at Jean and saw her begin to relax and felt himself doing the same. Donovan was something of a fanatic, obviously, an obeyer of orders without question, a my country-right-or-wrong type and an organic weapon which was always loaded and had only to be pointed at his country's enemies and turned loose. But he was also emerging as a human being, a man who did not, apparently, like scaring people half to death by pointing guns at them.

"I won't mention the project to you again," said Carson briskly, "but I will have to tell what I know to someone. It's important. I expect you're going to arrest us, take us somewhere for interrogation to clear up any doubts you may have about our allegiance. That will give me a chance to tell..."

Donovan was looking impatient and a little annoyed. He said, "You weren't listening to me, Mr. Carson. I am all alone, I cannot arrest you and I don't have the facilities for incarceration or interrogation. I'm sorry."

Carson swallowed and said, "Herbie Patterson?"

Donovan nodded.

There had been a few times in his life when Carson had been really afraid, but they had been nothing compared to this. His stomach was one hard, sick knot of panic, and saliva suddenly flooded his mouth, the way it sometimes did during a very bumpy flight and he started thinking about brown-paper bags. He wondered if it would hurt very much and for how long. No death, he was sure, was really instantaneous. He thought of the heavy caliber bullet smashing into his face, plowing through his brain. He thought of what another just like it would do to Jean's serious, finely-boned, lovely face.

139

Sweat trickled down his forehead, cheeks and neck like fine, cold raindrops and he could not talk. He tried to say something, anything, that would stop or even delay for a few minutes what was going to happen. But his mind, like the small, tight circle of the gun-barrel which threatened them, was going around and around screaming *No . . !*

"But we aren't spies, Mr. Donovan," Jean said desperately. "We, that is, he stumbled on this almost by accident and felt that it was his duty to protect it—"

"If I believed you both innocent, which I don't," said Donovan, "it still would make no difference. This project, I have been told, is too big for innocent bystanders to be considered important. I'm sorry."

He sighed, then went on, "This will have to appear as a normal, understandable crime, of course—the murder of a girl followed by the suicide of her lover, something like that. I can set the stage afterwards. If there does happen to be a third party hiding in the flat, that would complicate things—but I'm not really concerned with what the local police do or think.

"But there will be no unnecessary suffering," he added. "That is why I see no point in prolonging the agony . . . "

The gun moved slightly and Carson realized that he had only seconds to live and that Jean had even less. Abruptly a cold fury shattered the tight circle of panic in his mind.

"Don't be so blasted considerate! Give youself a minute to think, damn you! Just suppose we *are* spies. As the sole guardian of this most important of all projects, you should wonder who we pass our information to and if it is still possible to stop it getting out of the country. You should at least question us to see if—"

"I am required to give local protection only," said Donovan impatiently, "and trying to find out how you pass on information would involve other intelligence departments and a large number of people, which would advertise to the other side the fact that something is going on. This is a very small project. Officially it does not exist. I hope you haven't passed on any vital information. If you have, the only thing I am allowed to do is remove the source."

The small double circle of the barrel and silencer seemed to fill the whole world. It *was* the world and while he looked at it he could not think.

Carson jammed his eyes closed and said desperately, "You are in charge of local security, right? Suppose I tell you that you've fallen down on the job, that someone has penetrated your security blanket, that someone has ripped such a great big hole in it that Jean and I were able to walk in behind him without even having to stoop? Would you listen to me while I performed *my* patriotic duty, as you are performing yours, by telling you how it was done and who the enemy agent is?"

He opened his eyes then and saw that he was at last getting through to Donovan. Professional pride and patriotism were the weak spots. Angrily, the shadow security man said, "You're trying to wreck the project by suggesting that one of the engineers is a spy! That is a very old trick, Mr. Carson. But my job is external security—they handle their own recruiting. At the same time I have seen to the destruction of all paperwork and everything that could possibly show that anything at all was going on . . . "

"I know how well you covered up," Carson broke in, "and that you had no say in recruiting. But this agent was invited into the project—it was all set up so carefully and so long ago that they had no choice but to invite him in. They needed a guinea-pig, you see, preferably one with no known next of kin. And stop jabbing that thing at me! You are in charge of project security, yes? Are you going to guard the outside of the apple barrel while one rotten apple ruins the lot? Is that how you do your job, Donovan?"

Before the other could reply, Carson went on. "No matter what you do to us here, you must tell Daniels what I've told you. And don't worry, the project won't be wrecked by the top man having suspicions about one of his guinea-pigs. We were so sure of our facts that we were going to Daniels ourselves in a day or so. If you let us talk to Daniels now I can tell him exactly how it was done and, more important to the security aspect, when the information is likely to be passed on as well as the method. That's right, the project is still secure—for a few days, anyway. I can even tell him these things in your hearing without making you unhappy by discussing the project in detail . . . "

For a long time there was no response. Donovan's face was composed again, his anger gone, his brain working coolly and suspiciously like a good security man's should. Finally he nodded, lifted the phone with his free hand and put it to his ear. He said, "You dial, Mr. Carson, and I'll check that you get the right number. And be very careful . . . "

Twenty minutes later they left for Daniels' house in Carson's car, but not before Donovan had toured the flat with them checking wardrobes, cupboards and under beds for a possible third party. On the way they were very careful in what they said and did because Donovan sat in the back seat, constantly reminding them that nothing had changed and that they had been successful only in buying a little time. They tried hard not to believe him.

Chapter 18

They talked for a long time amid the tomatoes in Daniels' lean-to greenhouse. On three sides the glass streamed with condensation, effectively hiding them from outside observation, but the large pane in the door opening into the back of the house, because the kitchen and greenhouse were close to each other in temperature, was perfectly clear. It showed Jean and a little behind her Donovan, keeping his eyes and gun on both of them from a point where he was in no danger of overhearing anything that was being said.

While they talked the nearest Daniels ever came to looking Carson in the face was when he occasionally fixed his gaze on the knot of Carson's tie.

"Joe," said Daniels finally, still without meeting his eyes, "I believe that you and Jean Marshall are not agents of the other side, that you got into this through the highest motives and that John Pebbles is who you say he is. I'm grateful to you, and maybe a little angry as well for the spanner you've tossed into the works—but it isn't personal. The point I'm trying to make is this: Since Donovan brought you two here over an hour ago, your situation hasn't really changed."

Daniels' tone was regretful, sympathetic and somehow aloof, and these feelings were reflected in his thin, ascetic's face. Plainly he was concerned with the project as a whole and could not allow himself to become involved in individual problems.

Carson swore under his breath, thinking of the incredible violence of the peace demonstrations he saw practically every week end on TV. There was nothing so ruthless as a militant pacifist, and the mistake he had made was in thinking that there was any difference at all between Donovan and Daniels. It was an effort to keep his voice steady as he spoke.

"We aren't traitors, you know that, so I thought that we might join your project. I've already shown that you can use some help on the security side—"

"There can be only one security man. I'm sorry."

"But he doesn't even know what he is protecting. I do . . ."

"You don't, Joe," Daniels broke in again. "You have worked out a vague theory, accurate enough to make you realize the terrible consequences to the world if what we are doing here became general knowledge too soon, but you *don't* know what the project is about. I know you two are not traitors, just patriotic, innocent bystanders who unfortunately—"

"We came into this thing because of our interest in Pebbles," Carson tried again. "I'm certain that he hasn't been contacted by his people yet, and this gives us—Dr. Marshall and myself, that is—a chance to work on him before that happens. His conditioning is breaking down, we will be able to find out a lot about the other side's methods and why Pebbles was chosen for the job. Don't forget that he is not a trained spy but a top test pilot tipped, if what the magazine caption says is true, for cosmonaut training who was suddenly converted into a sleeper. Why was he planted in Hart-Ewing, where we haven't had a really secret project since the war? Was it sheer accident? Were they intending to plant agents like this in all the big companies and we happened to be first? Oh, I know that it was made to look as if you invited him in, but that is because the people who planned it are real

144

smoothies. It seems to me that he was tailored to fit your ultra-secret project. Doesn't that suggest anything to you?

"The point *I'm* trying to make," Carson ended, "is that they must know something about the project to be able to train Pebbles for it, or they have a similar project to which Pebbles belonged . . . "

Daniels' mind seemed to be miles away—like Donovan, he was probably not even listening.

"But I suppose," Carson added bitterly, "to avoid complications you will treat him the same as Jean Marshall and myself—elimination by Donovan's silenced cannon . . . !"

"Pebbles is far beyond the range of Donovan's cannon," said Daniels seriously, "and you have made a very strong point. But you must appreciate my position, too. When I went to the top man with my ideas for hiding the project even from our own counter-espionage people, I had to accept one rather fanatical watch-dog and keep a tight control on the number of project personnel. There is just no room for advisors or assistant security officers. But do you really care what happens to Pebbles?"

"I think so," said Carson. "He doesn't know that he is a spy, so at the moment he is just another innocent bystander like myself."

"And like yourself," said Daniels, "he doesn't really know what the project is all about . . . "

I'm losing, thought Carson. But he could not think of another argument that would have any likelihood of influencing Daniels and he was about ready to beg for his life . . .

" . . . We have one guard-dog," Daniels was saying, "but nobody in charge of internal security. I thought there was no need, you see. The project is staffed by personal friends or people I considered quite safe. None of them know about Herbie Patterson's death or of what could happen to you two—it would only bother them. I *still* trust my own judgment about them . . . " It was hard to read his expression, Carson thought, but it was obvious that some sort of battle was going on in the frigid reaches of that brilliant and emotionless mind. " . . . and your argument convinces me that we need Dr. Marshall's abilities more than your own. It also convinces me that the project needs another, and more trustworthy, guinea-pig.

"I'm afraid that is our only vacancy, Joe."

He stopped, waiting. Carson realized suddenly that he wasn't going to die—at least, not for a few days. He remembered Tillotson and wondered if the same thing, whatever it was, would happen to him. It was stupid of him to feel so elated.

"I accept," said Carson, and added, "even though it is simply a matter of time—"

"That's right," said Daniels drily.

" . . . before whatever happened to Wayne Tillotson happens to me. But thanks, anyway."

Daniels shook his head. "Wayne was unlucky. You will find it much safer being a patriotic guinea-pig than a patriotic innocent bystander."

"I'm beginning to dislike the word 'patriotic'," said Carson. "It has overtones of fanaticism and Donovan's disease. Couldn't I be an intelligent, self-interested guinea-pig?"

"No," said Daniels, smiling for the first time and looking him straight in the eye. "If you've taken this job, you aren't intelligent."

Jean and Donovan were called into the greenhouse a few minutes later, but it took nearly twenty minutes before the security man put away his gun. After that he drove Jean and Carson to the doctor's home to pack and explain her forthcoming three weeks' absence to her family and, by letter, to Hart-Ewing. Then it was Carson's turn to do the same, although in his case it meant writing notes to Bill Savage in Personnel, the owner of the flat and the milkman. They returned then to Daniels' house to wait until it was time to catch the first plane out, which would be in only a few hours.

It had been impossible to tell what Donovan had thought about it all. He did not seem to care about individuals, one way or the other. Unlike Daniels, Carson

146

thought, who also had the fate of millions of people weighing on his mind—Daniels struck him as being the rare type who could not forget that the millions of people *were* individuals . . .

During the flight to the launching site Daniels told them all that they could talk about anything they liked so long as it wasn't the project. The only consolation that Jean and Carson had was that they were not alone in their frustration—two of Daniels' engineers, George Reece and Bert Parsons, who were accompanying them, were also being forbidden to express curiosity about the presence of the doctor and himself.

They arrived in the early evening when a rather ostentatious sunset was making a fiery backdrop to the towering silhouettes of the launching silos which were planted all over the landscape like a skyscraper city with claustrophobia. A few of the launching towers were dark, but the majority of them blazed against the darkening sky like rectangular Christmas trees.

It looked as if their curiosity would be satisfied at last when they reached a small office opening off a partially manned control center and Daniels offered them seats. But it was one of the engineers, neither of whom had been offered seats, who asked the first question—or tried to.

"What are *they* doing h—"

"They are joining us to help with some of the, ah, psychological problems which have come up," said Daniels quickly. "They are not fully informed as yet so a discussion at this stage would only confuse them. As well, Joe, here, may be making a plus and minus trip shortly, and I would like him to get as many answers as possible from me . . . "

As the two engineers left the office Carson thought that their expressions as they looked at him were much too respectful to be reassuring.

Daniels cleared his throat and said briskly, "I'm going to be as fair as I can with you two by giving you complete and accurate information on effects while saying nothing at all about causes. There are several reasons for this. One

147

is that I believe in supplying only enough information to allow a man to do his job properly, another is that a large number of people working on or attached to the project do not know what it is all about. Yet another is that the causes which bring about the effects we are trying to control and use are not clear even to us.

"Well, Joe, what's the first question?"

Carson's mind had been seething with questions all day so that he did not know where to start. He was a little ashamed when the first question to occur to him was a purely selfish one concerning his own future. He said, "What happens to us now?"

Daniels smiled and said, "Nothing much until tomorrow when I want you to experience some prolonged negative G. You will be with a plane-load of would-be astronauts getting used to the feeling of weightlessness, and your cover will be that of an aviation journalist collecting material for an article. Dr. Marshall can go along, too, if she wants to, as a medical observer. I don't want either of you to talk to Pebbles until we're nearly ready to bring him back, which will be just before you leave, Joe. Until then there is very little you can do except stay from under our feet and prepare for your next contact with Pebbles."

"Weightlessness," said Carson, his centers of curiosity temporarily paralyzed by the implications. He was going to be a space-going guinea-pig . . .

"What I don't understand," said Jean suddenly, waving at the control center and the launching complex beyond, "is how you keep *this* a secret. And what about the expense?"

Carson heard Daniels' answer although he was not really listening to it. There was something about an agreement made during his original presentation to the top man. In addition to the highly unusual security arrangements the project was to have unlimited funds which would be made available from the defense budget by an extremely circuitous route. As for keeping the control center and launching pad secret, there was no need to.

148

Space travel these days was nothing to get excited about so far as the public were concerned. The only times that the press and TV people took an interest was when something unusually ambitious was being planned or someone got himself killed. There were so many different chunks of hardware being heaved into orbit these days, from communications and weather satellites to the bewildering variety of instrument and biological research packages sent up by the universities trying to satisfy their respective and highly specialized curiosities, that nobody was really interested.

There was so much going on all the time that eavesdropping was not worth the effort—it would be like trying to listen in and isolate all the conversations going on in the main concourse of a busy railway or air terminal. By taking a few simple precautions they could communicate with their vehicles with an infinitesimal risk of being overheard . . .

" . . . And in any case," Daniels ended, "so far as outsiders are concerned, our vehicles are not manned."

"Training," said Carson suddenly. "I can fly—a light aircraft, after a fashion—but an astronaut has years of training to—"

"It wouldn't matter," said Daniels, "if you were a junior assistant in a shoe store—except that flying training should keep you from becoming too disoriented and perhaps panicking. You will not be required to do anything. You won't be *allowed* to do anything but sit there . . . "

"There'll be a window?"

"You may look out the window as often as you like," said Daniels. "We don't want to take away all the fun . . . "

As he stared into the chief designer's eyes, Carson wondered why he did not simply grab Jean by the hand and light out of there. They could forget the project and Pebbles and the threat to the peace of the world—there was *always* a threat to the peace of the world, if not with confrontations or escalations or heightenings of tension, then in some other fashion. They could lose themselves

149

in a city somewhere so that the lonely Donovan could not find them, and just live with the threat the way everyone else in the world had been doing since Hiroshima.

The trouble was that he did not want out of it, and the reasons for not wanting out were not the result of patriotic feeling, concern for mankind or even concern for his own precious skin—they were simply stupid!

For the chance of looking out of a window, which might very well get steamed up, anyway, he was going to risk his life. Daniels had been right. He was not being motivated by *intelligent* self-interest, and Carson felt terribly confused and angry with himself.

"If it's any consolation," said Daniels, who had been watching him closely, "Tillotson and Pebbles felt the same way . . ."

Chapter 19

Three days later they were able to talk to Pebbles from the control center. His voice sounded strange but this was not, the communications man assured them, due to distortion of the signal. It was plain to all of them that Pebbles was very seriously disturbed about something.

"If we say and do what we're supposed to," said Jean, looking at Carson, "I don't know how he will react. Out there he might do something which would wreck the capsule."

Carson looked at Daniels, who shook his head and said, "He has no control. But if it is possible to break his conditioning without going to the extent of making him a raving lunatic, to the point where we can find out how much the people who placed him know or suspect about the project, I would like you to try."

It would have made the job much easier if he and Jean could have seen Pebbles. But the camera, like all the other recording equipment in the capsule, would transmit only a few minutes before the start of the minus trip home, that instantaneous journey which occurred when Pebbles pushed the red button—or rather, Carson hastily corrected himself, when Control pushed it for him.

"Take it easy, John," said Carson. "What's troubling you? The dreams again?"

"Yes."

"You can talk freely, John," Carson said as the silence began to drag. "Jean and I have joined the project, too, and we've told Mr. Daniels about your mental . . . confusion. He understands. You can talk about the dreams."

"I'm still afraid to go to sleep. And Joe, I dream them even when I'm awake . . . "

"Go on. I haven't much time to talk to you. John?" There was no answer.

At a time like this he should be able to do more than talk, Carson told himself, and much more than listen. He should be able to offer a cigarette, give the other's arm a reassuring shake and vary the tone of voice to suit the man's reactions. He should at least be able to *see* Pebbles' expression. But the screens in the control center showed only views of a rocket being readied for launching with the information that the countdown was at one hour and twenty minutes.

"John, listen to me!" he said urgently. "We have been thinking about you very seriously and we have come up with a pretty good theory. We no longer think that you were retarded—we believe that you represent a simple, if rather drastic, case of amnesia *which is beginning to pass*. That would explain the confused dreams *and* the speed you have learned—or rather, relearned—things recently.

"You see," he went on, "the best way to cure amnesia is to surround the patient with familiar objects, places and people. You, over the past few years, have gradually surrounded yourself with familiar objects, situations and, in a manner of speaking, places—but your cure is still not complete because the familiar faces were absent as well as the *voices* of your friends . . . "

There was still no response. Daniels was staring intently at Carson and so was Jean. Her expression warned

152

him that if he wasn't careful he would say or do something which would make them both ashamed of him.

But I like Pebbles, he raged at her silently, and aloud went on, "To be able to pick up things as quickly as you did, especially in a highly technical area like this one, you had to have prior knowledge and training. *Nobody* learns to fly as quickly as you did!

"We can only believe that all this was familiar ground to you, John," Carson continued, "and that you have done something very like it before. But something happened—some kind of accident, perhaps, although we know that it did not involve physical injury—and you forgot everything. But now we want you to remember. Try hard, John. We think you may already have been a member of a project very like this one. Try, please, to remember what happened and everything you possibly can about it, because if you do you can help yourself a lot. You can help us, too. And me, John. You can help make it safer for both of us because I'm going out there, too . . . "

"You? Joe, is it a . . . a minus trip?"

"So they tell me," said Carson, laughing, "but that is all they'll tell me. I only want to look at the view."

"It's worth seeing, Joe. Even though I think . . . No, I'm sure that I've seen it before . . . "

"That's it! Keep trying to remember. You were involved with a project like this one before your . . . accident. We're pretty sure of that. Try to bring it back. Your memories could help us, keep us from making mistakes, perhaps. We're your friends . . . "

"My other friends killed me! Do you hear that? They didn't want to and . . . and they didn't know they were going to do it, but . . . but they killed me, obliterated me, wiped me out! In the dreams it is always going to happen and it did. They didn't know

153

about it and I can't remember it happening, but it must have—no, it did happen!

"Now you are going to kill me, too."

"But, John," Jean said gently, "you are still *alive* . . . "

"We won't kill you," Daniels broke in fiercely. "You'll be safe, as safe as anyone could be in these circumstances. Wayne Tillotson died because he lost control of himself and his ship. You do not have control so you cannot . . . "

Daniels broke off. The voice pouring out of the speaker did not sound quite sane and the project chief knew that he was wasting his breath. Carson looked across at Jean, wondering if this was the proper time to detonate their psychological bomb, but the way her fingers gripped the tape spool gave him her answer. Daniels reduced the volume to a whisper and turned to them.

"Get out of here, you two," he said harshly. "Doctor, you can listen and talk to Pebbles from my office. Joe, you can do the same—and talk to me, if you have to—from the gantry. I'm sorry, but you'll have to leave, *now* . . . !"

"But Pebbles isn't due to push the button until early tomorrow . . . " began Carson, then shrugged. They were most decidedly not wanted in the control center just now, and curiosity over the reason why was eating at him like a duodenal ulcer, but he knew better than to waste his breath asking questions.

But he had been able to catch a few words here and there from the men who were beginning to fill the room, enough to know that they were setting up for a re-entry. But who else, beside Pebbles, was out there?

On the way out to the gantry curiosity got the better of him, but he could get nothing from Reece or Parsons except reassuring smiles—not, that was, until they walked past the door labeled "Dressing Room" and into the elevator. Then he asked a question which, so far as he was concerned, demanded an answer.

"What about my space suit?"

"You don't wear one," said George Reece. "This will be a purely shirt-sleeve exercise all the way. Besides, this way it is easy to make people believe that we are sending up an instrument or biological research package—they don't really notice or make a count of the comings and goings of people in sweaters and slacks if their IDs are in order. But if you were dressed in a space suit they would certainly notice *that*. Does the thought of not having one bother you, Joe?"

Not as much as the thought of Donovan, Carson replied silently, then aloud, "How long will the trip last?"

They did not answer that one. Carson began to lose his temper.

"Both of you travelled here with me," he said sharply. "You heard me trying to question Daniels, you heard him tell me that I could have full information on effects but nothing on causes. Play fair."

"A day or maybe less, Joe," said Parsons. "It all depends."

"On what?"

"We can't tell you," said Reece, "without discussing causes."

"Look," said Carson patiently, "I got into this mess because I have already found out a lot about the project. For instance, I'm pretty sure that neither Pebbles nor myself are going into a six- or seven-day orbiting session. Where am I going exactly?"

"To a point in space more than half-way to the orbit of Mars and three million miles or so below the orbit of Earth and angled towards the present position of Jupiter. Now are you happy?"

"What do I find there?"

"Nothing at the moment . . ." began Parsons, and stopped suddenly because Reece was glaring at him.

"So I'm going to rendezvous with someone, or something?"

"You could say that."

Before Carson could devise another question the elevator reached capsule level and he was hustled politely out. Reece opened the large canvas bag labeled "Waste" that he had been carrying and produced a set of one-piece

155

coveralls with zippers at strategic positions and a pair of light, rubber-soled boots. The maker's labels had been removed from everything. While Carson stripped and changed, the clothing in which he had arrived was rolled up and rammed tightly into the canvas bag.

"We'll have them cleaned and pressed for you by the time you get back," said Parsons, then added, "You know where everything is and how to use it. Any questions?"

"Are you kidding . . . ?"

But Carson was not, at that moment, thinking of questions. Instead he was staring at the capsule which projected through the hole in the center of the floor with its hatch open. He noticed, but did not seem to want to think about the fact, that there was no escape tower—an 'unmanned' capsule would not have one, of course. He kept thinking how familiar it was, remembering the times he had wriggled into one just like it in Engineering Test for a twenty-minute daydream of being in orbit. He thought that the butterflies indigenous to his stomach had grown to the size of blackbirds and he felt overwhelmed by an intense and fearful anticipation with, he thought, the fear just slightly less intense than the anticipation.

His curiosity, temporarily submerged, was still fighting to get to the surface . . .

"The rendezvous point," said Carson. "If it isn't chosen at random, and it can't be if I'm to meet something there, what factors dictate the choice of that position? Why that particular point in space?"

He broke off, remembering some of the snippets of information he had been able to pick up and overhear. He wondered suddenly if he had all the factors already in his possession. He went on, "Let me think a minute. Is the rendezvous point a product of three velocities acting in different directions? One of them is one thousand and thirty-four miles per hour, one is . . . is eighteen point five miles per second and the other is two hundred and fifteen miles per second . . . "

"Let me help you in," said Parsons. Reece said, "Make sure the harness is tight." The sudden lack of expression in their faces was answer enough. He had guessed right, but what exactly *had* he guessed?

"The way I see it," Carson went on as they checked his straps, "is that you send a vehicle to this predetermined point in space using conventional rocket power and several days to get there—just the way you've done with John Pebbles—whereupon the pilot presses the button on your hyperdimensional, interdimensional, spacewarp or whatever kind of drive it is that you've developed, and immediately he is back at home or at least in close orbit . . . "

From his position flat on the couch he could not see their faces and neither could he hear them. Both men had stopped breathing.

" . . . The question which then occurs to me is, why go the long way out and take the shortcut home? Why not push the button, that is, take the shortcut, in both directions? Or, to put it another way, what would be the *effect* of doing this? You're supposed to tell me about effects, remember."

When Reece answered several seconds later his voice sounded strained, almost frightened. He said, "We haven't tried a two-way fast trip until now because if the timing and positioning were not right the effects might be . . . well, anything from highly embarrassing for the guinea-pig concerned to completely and utterly disastrous to the universe we live in. But this time we're playing safe by boosting you into space before pushing any buttons. Does that satisfy you, Joe?"

"Now," said Carson numbly, "You're *confusing* me with facts . . . "

A few minutes later two hands appeared over his shoulder, grasped his and two voices wished him good luck. His ears popped as the hatch slammed shut.

"Minus twenty-seven minutes and counting," said the speaker just above his head in Daniels' dry tones. *"Are you comfortable, Joe?"*

"Yes," said Carson.

"Would you like to talk to Dr. Marshall?"

"Yes."

But when Jean came on he found that he could not say anything which was not utterly banal. Daniels murmured something about not wanting to intrude on what was undoubtedly going to be a tender farewell and he had work to do in Control, anyway. In the large fraction of a second that it took for him to open and close the office door behind him, Carson heard screaming. Or perhaps wailing would be a better description of the sound, because it seemed to be a product of distress rather than pain.

Tillotson was supposed to have made a noise like that during re-entry before his capsule burned up, but who was the third guinea-pig and what were they doing to him?

> *"I don't know, Joe. When I was talking to John Pebbles someone got the wires crossed for a few seconds and I heard it, too. All Daniels would say was that the man was safe, the capsule parachute has opened and been spotted by their private chopper and I will be going out in my professional capacity to the place they're taking him. He said to try not to let it worry you, Joe."*

"Hah!"

> *"He also said that I should use my discretion about telling you who the man is when I do find out."*

Carson waggled his head violently, trying to shake his brains into more effective thinking. He was sure that he now had all the important pieces of the puzzle, but they just would not fit together no matter how he moved them around. While he was still thinking hard the distant door opened and closed again and he heard Daniels say something quietly to Jean.

Maybe if he was given another piece . . .

"What about Pebbles?"

> *"Calmer now, but still confused. He hasn't said anything that you don't already know about the project or himself. Do you want to talk to him?"*

"Not yet," said Carson. "But try him with that tape, then let me listen to his reaction. Daniels? Can you answer one question? What are the effect—*effects*, remember—of your instantaneous space drive on human passengers . . . ?"

Several minutes dragged by, during which he heard Jean phoning to someone to bring her tape-recorder to the office, before Daniels replied. When he spoke he sounded guarded, worried and, so far as the listening Carson was concerned, not at all reassuring.

"You are very persistent, Joe. By now I would have thought that you had enough to think about out there, but since thinking is all you will be able to do I suppose it does no harm to confuse you further. The effects of what we call a plus trip on human beings and small experimental animals are negligible and quite painless. The effects of a minus trip on animals are also, we are pretty sure, painless. But there is a loss of physical coordination and severe mental confusion which lasts several weeks— in animals, that is. You will be the third man to make a minus trip.

"We had hoped that Wayne Tillotson, being much brighter and better coordinated than a mouse or a guinea-pig, would have been able to fight or throw off these effects and maintain control of his vehicle during re-entry or at least allow us to handle it from here if he didn't feel capable of it. With Pebbles and yourself we are taking no chances—you have no control.

"The effect of the drive, as you call it, on nonorganic material—the capsule, its systems and equipment, your clothing—is nil. On your body as a whole, not very much. But on your mind and nervous system . . . Well, even I am guessing here, but you have to realize that basically the 'drive' is a . . . a philosophical thing and it may well be that

159

*the Universe and the minds it contains are inter-
dependent . . ."*

Daniels laughed, not unkindly, and added,

*"That should be enough for anyone to think
about. You are at minus eight minutes, Joe."*

Before Carson could reply, Jean said,

*"I'm not sure that I approve of using this, but I
will . . . "*

The tape cut in at that point. It had been prepared by a
company who were not even remotely connected with
the project, so the things it said were general rather than
specific. But it dealt with everything Carson knew or suspected about Pebbles before, during and after his stay at
the Clinic and an unspecified industrial complex. It called
Pebbles by his real name and it was in Russian. In short
it was a psychological bomb designed to demolish an already weakened case of amnesia.

It exploded on target at precisely minus fourteen seconds.

"Wait!" said Carson urgently. "I want to hear this . . !"

*"At minus eleven seconds! Turn up your gain,
Joe. Right up, so you can hear it above the sound of
the motors . . . "*

Carson turned up the volume as Daniels had suggested
until the voice sounded as though it would blow off the
hatch, then he had ignition and discovered that it was not
nearly loud enough. The combined racket of rocket motors and receiver made it difficult to think. He felt the
ship begin to creep into the sky, then pick up speed
until something big and strong and invisible was trying to
push him through the bottom of his couch . . .

The voices of Daniels and Jean blared in over the other

one saying *"It looks good, Joe"* and *"Safe home, dear,"* and then there was only the voice of John Alexei Ouspenskaya Pebbles talking fast and not very coherently in two languages.

Chapter 20

". . . And it was just like this project. Nobody knew what would happen exactly—the lab animals had not appeared to suffer very much more than a few weeks' mental confusion and their instinctive behavior patterns did not change. A man would be able to do much better, they thought, so I volunteered and they killed me, Joe. They wiped out my mind. Now I know what they did, from the memories of a week before they did it and my life since Nurse Sampson found me on the beach.

"They suspected that the minus trip would rewind some of the memory tape, but instead it was wiped clean. They didn't realize that a man's brain can't run backwards, so they killed my personality, memories, everything! They were my friends just like you and Jean and Daniels are my friends, and now you are going to kill me, too . . . !"

With great difficulty Carson inflated a chest which seemed to have a baby elephant sitting on it, and said, "But, John, you didn't die permanently. It took nearly five years but you got it all back . . . "

"I don't know that, Joe—I still can't remember

*very well what I was like. It has been a new life
since then, a different one—a different me. And now
I'm going to lose even that . . . !"*

The voice bellowing in his ear above the thunder of the
rockets broke into furious Russian for a few seconds before reverting to English.

*" . . . You can't do this to me again. Please. Don't
let them do it to me, Joe. Don't let them do it to
you—"*

Daniels' voice roared in.

*"I'm sorry, I can't leave you out there even if you
really wanted me to—the minus trip is the only way
of getting you back, now. You have only five
seconds, John. I'm sorry. At the speed the Galaxy is
spinning we can't delay—"*
"Joe! Jean! Don't let—"

Abruptly the voices ceased their bellowing. A few seconds later the second stage fell away and the weight left
Carson's chest. But there was an even greater load he had
to get off his chest.
"Daniels!"

*"I'm really sorry, Joe. All that was as much of a
surprise to me as it was to you—we need time to
think about it. But I didn't want anything to happen
that would . . . unsettle . . . you. But there is no time
to talk about it because in a few minutes you will
be—"*

"Shut up and *listen!*" said Carson furiously. He felt suddenly enlightened, horribly afraid, completely ashamed
of his part in the Pebbles business and angrier than he
had ever been in his life. "Daniels, listen to me! Daniels,
you are *not* going to sick Donovan on to John Pebbles. To

163

hell with security and your project—he isn't and never was a spy and I don't want him harmed by Donovan or any other—"

Jean's voice came in then.

"I'll see that nothing happens to him. But if he arrives back in the same condition as last time, he will scarcely be a security risk. And neither will you, Joe. Will they, Mr. Daniels . . . ?"

She sounded angrier even than Carson, and almost on the point of tears.

"No, Doctor, of course not. There would be no point now that we know the other side are working on it, too. They must have been keeping it just as secret from their people as we are from ours, and probably for the same reasons. But how Pebbles arrived on that beach, naked—Wayne did the first plus trip naked, of course, because we weren't sure of the effects clothing might have in those days and we wanted to play safe. Pebbles must have gone off course, splashed down close inshore, and sunk. Part of the capsule parachute was found further along the beach and the rest of it is either still attached to the sunken vehicle or it was carried away by the ebb. He must have remembered—or known instinctively— how to swim . . ."

Jean broke in,

"You will be able to remember something or . . . or someone . . ."

"I expect so, Doctor. But right now there is something you should think about Joe. You are not going the long way under conventional rocket power to the rendezvous point. Instead you will make an instantaneous plus trip to that point in space, then hang around for an hour . . ."

164

He made a noise which was probably meant to be a laugh.

" . . . to avoid, well, too many comings and goings. When we give the signal from here you will return, instantaneously, to orbit around Earth.

"In a way this is an honor, Joe. Usually we send them out only a few hours equivalent distance— five or six million miles, that is—on rocket power, which can take anything up to a week, before bringing them back with the yellow button. But you we are sending out for a full day, more than eighteen million miles, using the drive both ways.

"Wayne was scheduled to make the first plus and minus trip . . .

"If you look to the left of the big clock on the main panel—the one with the red and yellow hands —you will see a red and a yellow button. Between them is a counter registering seconds. When it reaches zero press the yellow button. There is no discomfort during a plus trip.

"It might help your morale a little if you pushed the button, Joe. But if you don't, we will."

Carson looked at the counter, which was flickering down through the one hundred and twenties, then out of the port. The scene was so much sharper, more awe-inspiring and beautiful than he had expected that he found himself growing a little calmer. He still doubted that the view was worth getting himself killed for, even if his body would not technically die. Then he began to wonder if he was not mad for having any doubts at all about a thing like that. Reluctantly he tore his eyes away from the scene outside and back to the counter.

His silence seemed to be making Daniels uncomfortable.

"What I don't understand is how the other side got onto this idea. Admittedly the journals and pa-

*pers which started me thinking along these lines were
available to them as well, but—"*

"There is a time for steam engines and a time for airplanes and now," Carson said bitterly as he reached for
the yellow button, "it is time-travel time . . . "

There was no discomfort, no sensation of any kind
other than the shock of surprise at seeing the Earth suddenly switched off and replaced by stars and a Sun which
was too far away. Carson had never felt so alone in all
his life.

Tomorrow, he thought, *is too far.*

It was not time-travel in the accepted Wellsian sense,
where a few decades of travel into the future placed the
time-machine and its operator in the same house and room
that he had left, but in an older, perhaps ruined version
of the same building, or where a similar jaunt into the past
materialized them on rough ground before the place had
been built. Time-travel stories of that kind had taken too
much for granted.

The present-day time-traveler had to be an astronaut
as well. When he pressed the big yellow or red button he
materialized in the past or future in exactly the same
point in space—but in the meantime Earth, the solar
system and the Galaxy had either moved on or had not
arrived there yet . . .

Earth rotated once every twenty-four hours to give it a
rotational velocity at the equator of over one thousand
miles per hour—Carson was not sure of the rotational
speed at the latitude of the launching pad—and, making
due allowances for the perturbrations caused by major-
planet gravitational effects, the Earth's orbital speed as it
circled the Sun was about eighteen point five miles per
second. Meanwhile the Sun and the millions of other stars
comprising the spiral arm of the Galaxy which it occupied
wheeled ponderously around the galactic center at a velocity of two hundred and fifteen miles per second.

Time-travel involved no spatial displacement. It was

just that everything in creation was moving in several different directions at once.

Carson could imagine the early experiments and the jubilation when one of the test objects—probably a radio transponder or similar instrument capable of signaling its presence over vast distances—vanished to appear again many millions of miles out in space. They would have thought that an instantaneous space drive was almost within their grasp and that the exploration of the planets and neighboring solar systems was only a few years off. Instead they had discovered a space drive which required conventional rocket propulsion to get out to or return from the time-travel point if the astronaut was not to return a mindless idiot.

Travel towards the future was safe, apparently, but into the past meant oblivion, personality death, a one hundred percent thorough brain-wash.

Why?

The question required a quick answer, but somehow the necessity for finding it did not drive Carson into a panic, make him lose control of himself or start pleading with Daniels to be let off the hook. Out here, amid all this grandeur, it seemed to him that any display of purely human weakness would be in impossibly bad taste.

He had always prided himself on his memory and very soon he was going to lose it completely. But before that happened he would use his memory to try to find the answer. With his newly-gained knowledge of what the project was really about, he cast his mind back, going over all the clues, the overheard conversations, observations and deductions. Somewhere in that mass of remembered material there must be an answer.

But more than anything else he kept remembering John Pebbles—in the flat, at work and in the club. A grown man with high intelligence and the mind and sense of wonder of a small boy. Pebbles had returned safely from one, and by now, perhaps two minus trips. Wayne Tillotson had made only one trip into the past and they had made the mistake of assuming that he might be able to

167

take control of his vehicle during re-entry and that he would have enough sense left not to touch anything if he did not feel capable of controlling it.

He remembered Daniels' crack about traffic congestion —too many comings and goings—and began to wonder about paradoxes. Normally a trip involved traveling conventionally for many days until the vehicle reached that pre-calculated point in space which would be in the desired number of hours in the future, then the yellow button would be pushed and Earth would materialize below— no paradoxes, no problems. But for a minus trip the module would travel back, again taking many days for the trip, to where the Earth had been a few hours *earlier*. In this case there would be a few hours when the pilot was both coming and going, that was, the last few hours of conventional travel before pushing the red button when he had already landed. But it was not an embarrassing paradox because the man concerned would not meet himself because he was in two very widely separated places at the same time. The real problem was that one of himself would be in no mental condition to worry about meeting the other.

The activity yesterday in the control center when he and Jean had been sent to an outer office to talk to Pebbles was because the other, amnesiac Pebbles had already been on the way in.

Carson himself, if everything had gone as planned, was already down there being fed and cleaned and nursed . . .

"Carson to Control," he said sharply.

He waited grimly for the reply, remembering some of the things Daniels and Pebbles had told him. The designer had stated that time-travel had no effect on mechanical or electronic devices, minimal effects on living tissue and quite drastic effects on the thought processes. Obviously the project people tried to avoid paradoxes, but they did not know what laws, if any, they were breaking because Daniels felt that the answer might lie in the soft rather than in the hard sciences.

John Pebbles had told him much more when he had

said simply that a human brain could not be made to run backwards.

Carson thought he had the answer now. There might even be a chance for him . . .

"Carson to Con—"

"Go ahead, Carson," Daniels replied.

"But remember to allow for the time-lapse between question and answer—even at the speed of light it takes a while for radio signals to make the round trip. You're pretty far out, you know."

"Is John Pebbles safe, and am I?"

Two hundred interminable seconds later the reply came.

"Both of you landed safely yesterday. It sounds as if you have it all figured out already, but you will want to ask questions, anyway. Fire away, Joe, this time I'll answer them all, fully and accurately."

Carson thought bitterly that Daniels had nothing to lose when he was going to forget everything, anyway, because when Carson pushed that red button and went back to yesterday the hour he had spent out here would be gone, it would never have existed so far as his mind was concerned. Aloud, he said, "I'd like you to tell me all you know about the physiological effects of forward and backwards travel in time. And up to now project security has kept you from having competent medical advice available. I would like Jean to hear this if she's there. It will help her to better understand her . . . patients."

Ten seconds later Daniels said,

"Jean is here—she has been up all night and now both of her patients are sleeping peacefully. As for the physiological effects you ask about, there isn't much else I can tell you. A man going forward twelve hours in time, and that is the farthest ahead

169

we've gone until your twenty-four hour trip yester-
day, doesn't suddenly need a shave or feel hungry or
want to go to the toilet. But when we send very short-
lived insects on similar trips, in both directions, they
showed definite signs of biological aging and reju-
venation, respectively, after trips into the future and
past. They did not appear to be troubled by sudden
hunger or thirst, their appendages had not grown or
shortened—they simply got older or younger.

"We don't know the reason for this, Joe, but we've
come up with some pretty wild theories. The one I
favor at the moment goes like this: Non-living ma-
terial objects show no detectable effects—a camera,
for instance, can be sent into the past or future, take
photographs there which we can develop and print
in the present. But the physiological effects are such
that we are beginning to suspect that physical age
may be imposed by the mind, because it is only the
mind which is seriously effected by time-travel. The
new material which we got from John Pebbles yester-
day supports this, but we still need to do some se-
rious thinking about it."

"I have been doing some serious thinking about it,"
began Carson, and stopped. For the first time since he
had looked up from his tape-recorder and seen Donovan's
gun filling the universe he was beginning to feel hope.

"Probably I am just fooling myself," he went on, "and
wishing out loud rather than talking sense, but how does
this sound? During a forward trip, which is instantaneous, the elapsed time of the journey is not recorded in
the conscious mind because nothing at all happened during that period—no impressions, no cerebration, nothing
whatever to remember. On a minus trip into the past it is
different—especially, as was the case with Tillotson and
Pebbles, when they went the long way out to the jump
point on conventional rocket power. Before they traveled
back in time they had spent many days in their modules,
observing, reporting, making decisions, remembering.

When *they* pushed the red button all these sensory impressions and memories were gone, ripped out; they had never happened.

"It is possible," Carson went on, "that this sudden unlearning process, this violent removal of several days' thoughts, impressions and memories with all their associated linkages produces a very severe mental shock—complete amnesia, in fact. Everything which went on in the mind during the period covered by the minus trip is lost forever because they never really happened so far as the mind is concerned, but the memories before this time-jump period still exist but, because of the mental shock, return only slowly and with great difficulty. This fits with what we know of Pebbles before and after his first minus trip . . . "

"*I think you've got it, Joe . . .*" began Daniels excitedly, reacting to something Carson had said ten seconds earlier, then stopped because Carson had gone on talking.

On the panel a few inches away the red hands told him that he had less than twenty minutes and the red button stared at him, a little like Donovan's gun. He was going to commit suicide in . . . sixteen minutes, and he wondered if there was any other way of getting back without effectively killing himself . . .

"I am hoping that my own case may be somewhat different," he went on quickly, "in that I did not come the long way out. The only thinking I have done which will be unlearned at the jump back took place during the hour I have been out here—an hour, remember, instead of several days as was the case with Tillotson and Pebbles. I am hoping that the mental shock of having this hour removed from my mind will be less than' that suffered by my predecessors. If this is so, my 'cure' should not take as long as John's did, either, because I expect to be surrounded by familiar things and people—people who know what has happened to me—from the start.

"The people who surrounded John Pebbles did not know what they were supposed to do and did not even speak his language."

Carson took a deep breath, then ended, "What do you think, Jean. Does all this sound reasonable?"

But it was Daniels who replied first.

"I think you have the answer, Joe! And you're damn right we'll take care of you and help bring back your memory as fast as we can. Jean has already started. Apparently there is a whole range of medication that could help . . . She will probably tell you about it herself. I've got to go to Control right now to oversee your minus jump. You have about ten minutes. See you. And . . . thanks, Joe."

Jean said, *"How do you feel?"*

Carson felt angry suddenly as well as afraid. She was treating him as a patient already. But then he *was* her patient already and he would remain her patient for months or years to come. All at once it did not matter to him that he was going to forget everything, if he could be sure of forgetting his need for her.

"I never wanted to be your patient, Jean," he said bitterly. "I was hoping for a less professional relationship."

It took much longer than two hundred seconds for the reply to come back. Then he heard her laughing, or rather making the strained, odd-sounding noise that a person makes who doesn't know whether to laugh or cry. She said,

"I know what I said about preferring healthy friends to sick patients, Joe. But please don't worry about that, I mean it. You are a special case and . . . and just because a baby has to be looked after for a while does not mean that it is sick . . . "

He had only a few minutes left and there did not seem to be anything else to say. Carson leaned towards the port and with his left hand near the red button he used his right to block off the glare from the Sun. He thought

172

about Jean and he stared at the spectacle outside, trying uselessly to print it and her indelibly on his mind. He thought that if something was to go wrong out here he could dive for all eternity without ever hitting the ground, but the thought did not worry him very much. He was too busy trying to remember everything that had ever happened to him and drink in all this splendor, the vast and incredible beauty of it all, because it was the last thing he would experience in his present life . . .

The counter said minus five seconds.

"Jean," he said very seriously, "Please don't let me forget you . . . "

Chapter 21

He felt very pleased with himself the day he learned how to make it light or dark at will by opening and closing his eyes. He did not know what day or light or dark or eyes were, or what was meant by opening and closing, but he could do it and it was great fun. Then a time came when it stayed dark whether he opened or closed his eyes. This made him feel angry and he cried. He did not at that time know what being angry or crying was, but he did it anyway and the light came on.

The faces of a man and a girl looked down at him. The girl put her hand on his forehead and began to stroke it. He did not know what man, girl, faces, hand and forehead were, either, but he could see and feel. He stopped crying.

"Are you sure he is all right?" said the man.

"Look at the way he is opening and closing his eyes," said the girl. "He's playing a game of some sort. That's a very good sign . . . "

The words and sights and sounds went into his mind and circled endlessly, looking in vain for a place to live. Without knowing how or why, he felt sure that later they would find a home and he would be able to remember what it was that he had seen and heard. And the next day when he discovered how to play with his fingers, the sight and sound and soft feel of the girl was very pleasing to him, even though he did not know what that meant, either.

* * *

They put him down on the floor and he found out how to roll about, crawl and walk by holding on to the furniture. He learned to eat off a spoon instead of sucking at a bottle. He looked forward to eating because it meant the girl putting her arm around his shoulder to hold him steady and he could push the side of his face against her. When she taught him how to hold and use his own spoon and sit at a table to eat, he cried at first. But then she diverted his attention by showing him the grass and flowers and trees at the bottom of the lawn and the clouds in the sky, and she demonstrated gently how the window glass could hurt his head if he tried to push through it. Or she would teach him how to go to the toilet by himself or play a game where he got in and out of complicated clothing . . .

But she always put her arms around him and held him close before he went to sleep.

He still did not know what the things were that he was experiencing, except between the times when he went to sleep and woke up. Then things happened which frightened him sometimes, but he thought he almost understood them.

Without knowing what mind and black and glass were, he thought of his mind as being behind a sheet of black glass. When he learned or saw or touched something new a tiny, shining hole appeared in the black glass with cracks of association radiating from it in all directions. He was sure that the things which were always happening around him should widen and lengthen the cracks, extend the associational network, link up those tiny, shining stars or knowledge.

He did not know what cracks and associational networks and stars and frustrations were, but stars made him feel excited and afraid and it was very frustrating not to know what it was that his mind was thinking about.

* * *

175

"No," said the sight-sound-smell-touch of the girl who was standing beside his chair with her hand on his head. "There is no real need for alphabet building blocks, or kindergarten teaching aids, or basic reading and maths. He should *remember* how to read, not have to have it taught to him all over again, even if he is a very fast learner. This time I'll begin with illustrated encyclopedias, aviation journals, samples of company paperwork. I'd like you to bring in a TV, and set up a projector and screen . . ."

"Rushing things a little, aren't you?" said the man on his other side, adding quickly, "I wasn't criticizing, Doctor. I know how you must feel these past few years."

"I wonder if you do," she said in a tone which made him want to put his arms around her and stroke *her* head. "And I'd like a tape-recorder, too, playing unobtrusively day and night. The usual tapes, of course—voices, his own voice, traffic sounds, factory noises, favorite music . . . "

His associations between the sight and sound of people widened dramatically after that. He could tell them apart and even try to form the sounds of the words they called themselves. There was only one girl and fourteen men. One of the men called himself Daniels and he was living in a thing called a room in Daniels' house. All the men took it in turns to watch and talk to him, and work the projector and change tapes and make sure he did not turn on all the faucets in the bathroom or fall downstairs again. The girl came much more often than the men and she was always there before he went to sleep or when he awakened from a bad dream. The number of holes in the black glass wall in his mind grew, but slowly and they very rarely linked up.

He listened constantly to meaningless sounds and the voices of people speaking gibberish, and at night he listened to the same people in his dreams and almost understood them. But the dreams were not always frightening. The girl was in some of them, talking to him sometimes or playing with him and doing things which he had

176

no words for and which made him very sorry to have to wake up.

* * *

Even though he knew that the TV set and the projection screen were not windows, it was easier to think of them that way. Today they were going to show mostly films, they had said, and both the girl and the man Daniels talked too loudly and dropped things during the preparations.

The first film showed a roaring, stiff-winged bird which he knew was called an airplane taking off, circling an airfield and landing after touching the ground three times. Two figures climbed out of it, one of which he recognized as himself and another which the girl called Pebbles. There followed a close-up of the cockpit, the dash, a still of Pebbles in the cockpit smiling at him . . .

Pebbles.

He felt suddenly frightened. Another hole was being knocked in the black glass wall in his mind and this time he did not want it to happen. There were too many cracks radiating from it, going in too many directions. On the other side of the room he could see, dim in the reflected light from the screen, the girl watching him. For a reason which he did not understand, but which seemed important to him, he forced himself not to cry or call out to her.

The sequence ended and was replaced by another showing Daniels and several of the other people he knew sitting at tables with colored lights on them. There was a deep, growling sound that he could feel in his stomach as well as hearing through his ears. Everybody was talking at once and the picture changed to that of a shining tower with fire belching from its base . . .

He tried hard not to be a cry-baby, to be what Daniels called a good soldier, but the film was knocking the biggest hole yet in his black glass wall and great, fat cracks were radiating from it in all directions, dividing and sub-dividing as they went. Some of them went towards the bright holes that were Pebbles and the factory and Daniels and

177

the girl. They were linking up, associating, with everything he knew or had learned, even his dreams, and he was very frightened. In that flaming, thundering monster he was going to die . . .

Whimpering, he ran towards the dimly seen couch which held the girl.

"Bingo!" said Daniels, very quietly.

It was a long time before they were able to calm him down, and then only after the girl had given him four tablets and Daniels had managed to pour enough water into his mouth to allow him to swallow them. But still he clung tightly to the girl, pressing his face against her, trying to hide from his own thoughts. "You shouldn't throw yourself at me that way," she said gently at one stage, "or hold me so tight. You're bigger than I am and the breaking strain of my ribs is low. But it's all right, I'm not angry . . ."

"What do you think, Doctor?" said Daniels.

"I think maybe . . . tonight," said the girl.

"Eleven days," said Daniels, "This time you did it in eleven *days*."

He felt himself relaxing and beginning to feel sleepy. He began to dream, one of the nice dreams with the girl in it where they did things he did not know the name of. The dream was so vivid that it woke him up. He was shaking and he could feel his body reacting and all he could do was stare wide-eyed at her without knowing or being able to say what was wrong.

"Now who's rushing things?" said Daniels, laughing.

Her face was pinker than usual as she said, "I think we should put you to bed now. I . . . I mean, mother love you can have, and welcome, but I don't think you are quite ready for the other kind . . . "

She sounded as if she might be asking a question.

* * *

He awoke several times that night and she was always there, wrapped in a man's dressing gown, watching him or stroking his head or talking quietly and soothingly. It got

178

so that he did not know when he was awake or asleep. She was always there, she had always been there—he could remember it happening before. He could *remember*. Suddenly he could see and hear and understand what he was seeing and hearing and remembering.

Pebbles . . .

Lavatory attendant, *Scheherazade,* the factory, the club, the flat, the picture in the aviation magazine, the voice saying *"You have control, Mr. Carson"* and *"Joe! Jean! Don't let them do it to me . . !"* and the voice of Daniels saying "Pebbles is an embarrassment to us, Joe, now that we know who and what he is. Not a threat, you understand—I'm not even thinking of using Donovan, because Pebbles lost much more than you did when you both came back that day. I'm . . . well, thinking of doing something very wrong. I'm going to send him home.

"It's obvious that they are hiding their project as we are hiding ours," Daniels had continued. "But there is only one man over there who could head it and I know how to contact him. I'll see that he finds out about Pebbles. We can say that he has been wandering around like an idiot—right now, after that trip, we won't have to lie about it—and that we only discovered his real identity from an illustration in an old magazine. He'll be taken into their project, cared for and eventually recover and be interrogated by our project's opposite numbers. They will be surprised and, I hope, delighted to get information from him on both projects. It might be enough to make the two non-existent projects join forces. We need a fresh viewpoint if we're ever to lick this time-travel problem.

"I've already mentioned my idea to the top man," Daniels had added. "He said I should be shot for being a traitor, but he didn't actually forbid it . . . "

When was that? Carson thought. *How old am I?*

Old, the red button, the trips never remembered because in *his* mind they had never happened. Daniels and the girl . . . Jean . . . talking, laughing, almost crying as she had said, "When is it going to stop? How many trips, how many years are you going to do this to him?"

"Soon, we hope," Daniels had replied. "We are beginning to get a feedback from our opposite numbers. They had been following a line which we overlooked, and vice-versa. I'd say that in two, maybe three years we will have instantaneous *space* travel, anywhere, with no time penalty. I realize the strain this puts on you, Doctor, but you are getting better and faster each time. And remember, we only forced him to go the first time—after that he was quite insistent about volunteering. He really wants to go out there, Jean."

"I know he does and I wouldn't think of stopping him. At times I'm quite proud of the idiot . . . "

There was a non-sound of mental gears crashing as Daniels tried to change the subject.

"I never suspected that time-travel would have cosmetic applications. You should try a trip yourself one day. I'm sure Joe would not mind returning the compliment and nursing you for—"

"Are you suggesting, Mr. Daniels, that I am beginning to look like a bag?"

"Oh, dear. How I manage to go on talking so clearly with my foot in my mouth never ceases to amaze me. I was only suggesting a theory to explain the absence of lines of worry, experience or wild living from his face, and his youthful air generally. We *know,* from the last trip but one, that he will live to a ripe old age. Is it possible that if the mind dictates and largely controls the physical condition of the body, then a regular mental spring-cleaning of this kind could have a very good effect on the . . . "

How old am I? Carson thought fearfully. *How many trips and how much time between them?*

In the seething chaos that was his waking and dreaming mind the answers came, not in single words and sentences but as sharp, bright, palpable incidents complete with dialogue. The tiny holes and cracks in that big black sheet of glass were barely noticeable now. Someone had heaved a brick through it and the light was pouring in.

" . . . This trip would, if you accepted it, involve drastic

180

rejuvenation and loss of experience," Daniels was saying. "You would arrive with the physiological age and body of a boy of six and the mental ability of, well, I don't have to go into that—let's just say that the only memories you would have available for recovery when you got back would be those you experienced between birth and the age of six, so that you would never be really normal again. Set against this is the fact that you would materialize within fifty miles of the surface of . . . "

"No."

"I don't blame you. But there are still some nice spots for you to visit on a plus jump. Three months from now we can place you two hundred miles from Mars and next week, if you agree and the ship is ready in time, within spitting distance of Ganymede. Then late next year—the planetary and stellar motions are so complex it will take us nearly that long to work out the exact position and timing—a jump of four months will put you very close to Pluto . . . "

There had been eleven trips. He had not and did not remember them, of course, because they had been wiped from his mind along with everything else during the minus jump back. But he had seen films taken by automatic camera in his capsule. They had shown all these wonders and many more, they had shown interstellar space far beyond the edge of the solar system when he had jumped, not a few days or months, but forty years ahead, and they had shown himself, middle-aged and sometimes older, looking eagerly at a view he would never remember. He heard as well as saw himself talking in his old, weak, excited voice as he described the view and taped instrument readings and carried out experiments ordered by the project engineers. Once the film had shown him dead.

That had been the result of a temporal over-shoot. Daniels refused to tell him how far into the future he had gone on that occasion because no man should be told even the approximate date of his own death. He could not remember that incident, either, so that another host of philosophical questions remained unanswered. The other questions and paradoxes they managed to avoid . . .

"I agree that it would be more economical to make the double journey from the Earth's surface, perhaps from the interior of a large hangar," he remembered Daniels saying, "but there are two very good reasons why we cannot risk it. One, it would be practically impossible to explain away a space communications link with associated equipment serving a vehicle which apparently never leaves the ground, and two, if there was the slightest error in timing or equipment malfunction we might have the vehicle arriving back before it had set off and trying to occupy the same space. The resultant explosion might wipe out the city, maybe even the country, and very likely give an accidental start to the final war.

"But one of these days we'll crack the problem, Joe. We're very close to doing it now. When this work started I thought time-travel was *more* impossible than instantaneous travel through space, and I still think so. We took the wrong turning somewhere. Even at two hundred and fifteen miles per second your life is only long enough to take you about one twentieth of the way to the nearest extra-solar planets. But don't worry, soon you'll be able to go to the stars and look around and remember everything when you come back. But right now you will have to be satisfied with being poor old Joe Carson, the chief security officer with . . . problems."

Poor Joe Carson . . .

He came fully conscious then, muttering and squirming in the bed and trying to get up. Immediately she was leaning over him, smoothing his hair and running her fingers along his cheek. Suddenly, but very gently, he reached up and drew her down until their lips met. For a few seconds she tried to pull free and then she spent the rest of the time trying to get closer.

It was coming back. All of it.

Poor Joe Carson, the man who had nervous breakdowns the way other people had head colds. Over-work was the reason, everyone said, and that was why the company was keeping him on and employing an assistant for him who really did all the work. Eleven breakdowns in four years, wasn't it? The first one had needed five months to recover from, but in recent years he was rarely absent for more than a few weeks. It was strange how healthy and happy he looked when he was well, then suddenly he would be gone again for more treatment. It was the Marshall girl they were all really sorry for. Joe Carson had married her after his first breakdown, probably working on her sympathy, and they had been a loving and devoted doctor and patient ever since. But the girl did not seem to mind.

No, thought Carson, *she doesn't* . . .

The black window was gone now, completely smashed. Even the odd pieces adhering to the frame had dropped away. He relaxed his hold on her just enough to give room for their lips to move and said, "This is the part I always like. The Princess Charming and the Sleeping Beast bit . . ."

Suddenly she was lying beside him and dripping tears all over his face. "Oh, Joe," she said, "Welcome home . . ."